One-Man
Massacre

Also by Jonas Ward
in Large Print:

The Name's Buchanan
Buchanan's War
Buchanan Gets Mad
Buchanan's Revenge

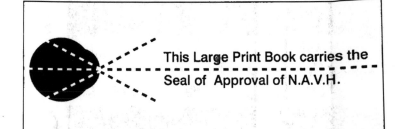

This Large Print Book carries the
Seal of Approval of N.A.V.H.

One-Man Massacre

Jonas Ward

Published in 2005 by arrangement with Golden West Literary
Agency.

Wheeler Large Print Western.

The text of this Large Print edition is unabridged.
Other aspects of the book may vary from the original edition.

Set in 16 pt. Plantin by Al Chase.

Printed in the United States on permanent paper.

Library of Congress Cataloging-in-Publication Data

Ward, Jonas.
    One-man massacre / by Jonas Ward.
        p. cm. — (Wheeler Publishing large print western)
    ISBN 1-58724-961-8 (lg. print : sc : alk. paper)
    1. Large type books.   I. Title.   II. Series: Wheeler large
print western series.
PS3557.A715O54 2005
    813'.54—dc22   2005001332

One-Man Massacre

As the Founder/CEO of NAVH, the only national health agency solely devoted to those who, although not totally blind, have an eye disease which could lead to serious visual impairment, I am pleased to recognize Thorndike Press* as one of the leading publishers in the large print field.

Founded in 1954 in San Francisco to prepare large print textbooks for partially seeing children, NAVH became the pioneer and standard setting agency in the preparation of large type.

Today, those publishers who meet our standards carry the prestigious "Seal of Approval" indicating high quality large print. We are delighted that Thorndike Press is one of the publishers whose titles meet these standards. We are also pleased to recognize the significant contribution Thorndike Press is making in this important and growing field.

Lorraine H. Marchi, L.H.D.
Founder/CEO
NAVH

* Thorndike Press encompasses the following imprints: Thorndike, Wheeler, Walker and Large Print Press.

ONE

The little old man and the big young one sat side by side on the top of the mountain, faces turned thoughtfully toward the rugged Big Bend country directly below, backs disdainful of the magnificent sunset being staged over the whole state of Chihuahua.

They sat together without speaking, the one with his ancient and fragrant Meerschaum, the other with his diminishing sack of Bull Durham, and soon the moonless night began closing in on them and the mountain and all the borderland like some softly closing door. Then it was pitch black, and something he saw made the young one shift his wide shoulders restlessly.

"Damn it all, Fargo, you did it again," he growled.

Surprise made the old man's pipe glow brightly.

"Did what again, Buchanan?" he inquired.

"Lost track of another damn day."

"The hell you say!"

"Look for yourself, oldtimer," Buchanan told him and Fargo looked, looked straight down from the mountaintop. He shook his white-haired head incredulously.

"Now what can those pure fools be thinking of?" he demanded. "How come they to light up Scotstown of a Friday night?"

Buchanan sighed and ground his cigarette into the earth.

" 'Cause it's sure-as-sin Friday," Fargo continued positively. Then he snapped his fingers. "Say — I'll bet it's the Fourth of July!"

Now Buchanan laughed.

"Should of quit when you drew even," he suggested drily. "Now you've lost us a month."

"Ain't it July yet?" Fargo asked, doubt lining his voice.

"Not if we got here the middle of March. That makes it a Saturday, middle of June, give or take a week."

"Well I'll be damned! How come I to miss checkin' off a day like that?"

"Same way you misjudged the soft life of gold mining," Buchanan said.

"Not me, son. No, sir! I never claimed nothin' for mountain livin' nor mountain minin'."

Let it go, Buchanan thought wearily, remembering full well how the old man had showed him the dog-eared map in that El Paso saloon, the picture he'd painted of the two of them stuffing their pockets with nuggets the size of eagle eggs. What the fast-talking old faker was looking for in Paso was some two-legged jackass to break his back against a goddam mountainside sixteen hours a day. Meet Mr. T. Jackass Buchanan.

"We ain't doin' so bad," Fargo was telling him now. "Not bad at all. Betcha the stuff we got assays out to thirty, thirty-two dollars the ounce."

"Sure."

"It will! Don't you think Fargo Johns knows the pure dust when he gets it in his palm?"

"Hell, I reckon it's real enough, Mr. Johns. I just hadn't figured on spending the next fifty years of my life swinging your pickaxe."

"And you won't! You sure won't! Afore winter we'll have enough to sneak us twenty, thirty Mexicans up here. Just see if we don't. Then you and me, boy, we'll just sit on our duffs and straw-boss the whole shebang."

"Sure," Buchanan said. "Before winter."

The rebuff sent Fargo back to his pipe, lapsed him into troubled thinking. Nothing in this life comes easy, he argued to himself; then had to admit he'd never thought it would be this hard. Their take to date probably didn't amount to more than three or four hundred dollars — and something he'd been observing for the past few weeks augured worse for the future. Oh, the ore was there all right, plain as a wart on your nose. But though the mountain might be one pile of rich gold, getting it out was going to get rougher and rougher — too rough even for someone with the prodigious size and energy of his young partner. They badly needed waterpower, drills, three crews of Mexicans working round the clock.

The pipe went out, sending a bitter taste along the curved stem. Story of my life, he thought. Sixty-four years of it. Or was it sixty-five? Born July 18, 1782, he knew that much. And been hanging by my thumbs ever since.

Buchanan's great arm slipped around his thin shoulders.

"Don't mind my griping," Buchanan said. "Those town lights threw me off kilter."

"Man gets pretty fine-honed, livin' like this," Fargo conceded.

"Yeah. Go turn in, Fargo."

"Be some risky, droppin' down there for a visit," the old man said probingly.

"Some."

"Stranger in town, busybodies askin' him questions. Fella takes a drop or two too many and he starts braggin' about his gold mine."

"Right. Get your sleep, oldtimer."

"Rascals be scramblin' up our mountain like pack rats," Fargo continued. "Steal us blind . . ."

"Night, Fargo."

The old man got to his feet, stood looking down at the blocky figure of Buchanan anxiously. Even as the younger one was now, seated, motionless, he communicated a throbbing vitality, a wildness that was all the more felt because he was caged.

"Hell's bells!" Fargo burst out impatiently. "What harm can it do?"

Buchanan raised his chin. "Now what?"

"Go on down there for a couple hours. Let some steam off."

"Why don't we both go?"

"Me? Go all the way down this mountain in the black of night and back again just for some white corn?" He laughed scornfully at such a notion. "Catch me travelin' all that distance just to get cheated

11

of my hard-earned money."

"You're gonna talk yourself into the trip pretty soon," Buchanan commented.

"You couldn't take me there piggy-back," Fargo said resolutely, walking off. He returned in a few minutes carrying a small leather pouch.

"Don't throw it all away in one place," he said, passing the fifty-odd dollars' worth of gold to the big man. "And whatever you do, don't let no two-legged wolves follow you back up here."

"Bring you back anything?"

"Well, if there's some left over, buy me a little tobacco."

"That all?"

Fargo hesitated. "Got a birthday comin' up pretty soon, if I keep close track of the days. Might treat myself to a bottle of the mountain dew."

"See you in the morning," Buchanan said.

"Watch yourself, now."

"Sure."

"Hey, ain't you goin' to arm yourself?"

"Travelin' light," Buchanan said.

"Just as well," Fargo concluded. "Can't get into trouble without a gun."

Buchanan crossed the clearing and disappeared over the side of the mountain, strolling with the lighthearted air of a man on a lark. If the lights of Scotstown meant only five miles of hard traveling to Fargo, they promised his tall partner a few hours' reprieve from the lonely mountain life. The prospect of hearing just one other human's voice paid for the trip in full.

TWO

Gibbons was a man of not more than medium build, but his specially made boots and high-crowned white Stetson gave the impression of someone much taller. His entrance into the Edinburgh Hotel was impressive as well, the manner in which he strode directly across the small lobby telling all present that here was a man whose every waking moment was of urgent importance and significance. Following exactly one pace behind him, in pseudo-military fashion, were two lean-faced, bleak-eyed ones with the stamp of gunfighter all over them.

The man in the Stetson stopped at the desk, turned when the clerk answered his brief question by pointing to a group of men standing across the room, then walked that way in his brisk fashion.

"Do I have the honor of addressing Mr. Malcolm Lord?" he asked the heavy-set, hawk-nosed man in the center of the group.

"You do, sir," Lord told him formally.

"And you are Captain Gibbons?"

"At your service."

They shook hands then, and Malcolm Lord's eyes made an approving appraisal. He introduced Gibbons then to the other four — Butler, Watson, Sims and MacPike. Gibbons acknowledged each one ceremoniously, unsmilingly, then swung aside.

"Gentlemen, my aides — Sergeants Leach and Gruber," and by the act of turning his back to them in the next moment he spared the Lord party any further socializing with underlings.

"I suggest we adjourn to the Glasgow," Lord suggested. "We will have privacy there for our business." They left the hotel and crossed Trail Street to the noisy, brightly lighted Glasgow Saloon. Somehow the "sergeants" made their way to the head of the party and it was they who pushed open the swinging doors and entered the place first. And somehow the way they paused just inside the doors, hands hooked above high-riding gun butts, brought a hush in the sound, sent a warning to every man in the big room. They moved to either side then and let the group come in.

"This way," Malcolm Lord directed, leading them to the private room he had reserved for the evening.

15

Suddenly a voice cut through the semi-silence from the direction of the long bar. "So that's Black Jack Gibbons!" it said belligerently, colored perhaps by whisky, but far from drunk. "Feast your eyes, gents — there's the man that claims full credit for the Brownsville massacre!"

Leach and Gruber had closed in instantly around Gibbons, who had stopped in his tracks at the first sound of the quarrelsome voice.

"Good company you're keeping, Malcolm Lord," the speaker went on. "The Rangers couldn't stomach him after Brownsville, but I guess that don't hold for you."

"You're sodden drunk, as usual, Angus Mulchay," Lord snapped back across the room. "One more insult to my guest and I'll forget your weakness . . ."

"No you won't," the man named Mulchay answered. "You'll get somebody else to do your fighting, just as you've imported this butcher . . ."

"No," Gibbons said curtly to Leach when the gunman had started toward the bar. "Not here."

". . . and I'm onto you, Lord," Mulchay continued. "You've been raising a big bogeyman about Mex bandits for months

16

now. But you don't fool me or any of the rest of us on the riverside. We know what you're after, and by God we'll fight you tooth and nail!"

"Whatever I do is for the benefit of us all," Lord said, addressing himself to everyone present. "For Scotstown and for the Big Bend." With that he started again toward the door of the private room.

"For the benefit of Overlord!" Angus Mulchay shouted after him. "You won't stop till you own it all!"

The door opened and the party went on through. Gibbons stopped briefly on the threshold.

"No one else comes inside," he told his men. "And avoid trouble with that loudmouth. This deal isn't set yet."

"I was fixin' to cut the dust some," Leach said, his manner truculent by nature. "It's a long ride from Lajitas."

Gibbons studied him, his small mustache bristling, and in his mind he was weighing Hamp Leach's ability with a gun and Hamp Leach's talent for making himself unpleasant. The gun won.

"Take your pleasure, Hamp," he said. "How're your funds?"

"What funds?"

Gibbons took a thick wallet from his coat,

17

extracted two twenty-dollar gold certificates and gave one to each of them.

"Go easy, boys," he cautioned. "The treasury is feeling a pinch." He went on in and Leach left Rig Gruber to guard the door while he himself sauntered to the bar. He did not move to where the garrulous Mulchay still held forth — not because Gibbons had ordered it, but because of someone who had caught his eye at this end. She was tall for a woman, taller than many men, and her long, raven-black hair and piquant Scotch beauty lent an air of tamelessness about her. Barmaids in Hamp Leach's considerable experience were either overly shy or overly bold, but this one carried herself with a kind of quiet dignity, as if this were a profession to be proud of. Leach knew different. Border women doing this work had descended to it, and every one was a wench for the asking.

"The best in the house, honey," he told her, leaning his loose-jointed frame far over the bar, bringing his high-cheekboned face familiarly close to the girl's. Now he stared insolently down the neck of her dress, and each thing he did was the sure-footed, no-nonsense approach that had never failed him from El Paso to Brownsville.

"Put your leerin' mugg back on its own

side of the stick," Rosemarie MacKay told him, enough of the burr and the heather in her voice to indicate she hadn't been transported across the ocean too long ago.

"Watch yourself, dossie," Leach cautioned. "I'm not one of your two-bit cow chasers." His glance fell again to her queen-size bosom and rested there for another disrespectful moment.

The girl took a step backward, her mind flashing a warning. He was a different proposition from the men who came to the bar and flirted with her in their half-shy, good-natured way. There was evil in this one.

"What will you have?" she asked as neutrally as she could manage.

"Like I told you, baby — the best in the house."

"We have Scot's whisky and corn. Beer in the keg, but no ale tonight."

"You got a sister over in San Antone? Half-breed?"

"Whisky or beer?"

"Set up along your general lines?" Leach went on, his eyes taking another long journey. "And friendly to a fighting man."

"The friendship here is in the glass," she told him, then started to move away.

"A bottle of the corn," Leach ordered, his voice abruptly turned surly. She lifted a

19

quart bottle from the back bar, uncorked it and set it in front of him with a glass. Suddenly his powerful fingers snaked forward, much too quick for the girl to retract her hand. His grip closed harshly around her slim wrist.

"Listen good, dos — you're doing business with Hamp Leach . . ."

"Let go of me."

"Or what?"

"Or I'll call for help."

Leach, still holding fast, cocked a derisive glance over his shoulder. Ranchers, punchers, clerks and barflies — typical cowtown gathering on Saturday night. The young bucks might come to the Glasgow later, but not until they had kicked up their heels to every jig and reel at the dancehall down the street.

"Call," Leach invited, but she had seen the same faces in the crowd he had, knew them all for basically good men but certainly no match for this professional trouble-maker.

"Please let me go," she said.

"What's goin' on?" a voice demanded, and it was the self-same Mulchay, two drinks older than he had been and making his way recklessly along the bar.

"Watch yourself, Angus." A friend tried

20

to caution the little terrierlike rancher, but he might just as well have warned a cock let loose in the pit.

"Take your mitts off that lass!" Mulchay demanded, coming to an unsteady halt. A wicked smile signaled Leach's intentions just a bare instant before he brought a heavy-booted foot from the floor, planted the heel deep into the older man's belly and kicked out with it. With a sickening grunt Angus Mulchay was jolted backward into a table and down. He lay there for several seconds, fighting for breath, then rolled to his hands and knees and started to rise again.

"No, Mr. Mulchay," Rosemarie cried to him. "Don't!"

Mulchay got to his feet, weaving from side to side, and Leach, smirking at the man's determination, slid the .45 from its holster and flipped it easily so that he held it by the long barrel.

"Come on, Angus-boy," he said goadingly. "Step up and get your thick skull split open."

The words were spoken into a heavy silence that had fallen over the big room. Mulchay eyed the weapon steadily, and so deep was everyone's concentration that no one heard the batwing doors swing wide to admit another spectator.

"Come on, Angus," Leach invited again, his voice thick with the desire to inflict pain. "Come and get it, cowman."

Mulchay passed a hand across his mouth and stepped toward him, recklessly. Leach's arm swept back — and then a huge shape shouldered itself between the two of them.

"If you're not too busy, ma'am," Buchanan said to the wide-eyed Rosemarie, "I'd sure like a drink."

"Get the hell outa my way!" Leach snarled, and Buchanan turned with a look of surprise. Now his shoulders blocked Mulchay off completely.

"If I'm in your way, brother," he said amiably, "then walk around me." His attention returned to Rosemarie and the sight of her made him smile. "If it wouldn't be too much trouble . . ."

Leach swung at his head and Buchanan picked off the blow with his left hand, forcing the gunman's arm up.

"What's biting on you, anyhow?" he asked him in a conversational tone, peering inquisitively into the taut, white-with-rage face of the other man. With all his strength Hamp Leach jerked to free his arm. Buchanan held fast, then twisted the gun out of Leach's fist and sent it skidding the length of the bar with a lazy motion. He turned to

Rosemarie for the third time.

"Now, ma'am — how about that drink?"

The girl blinked her eyes and swallowed. "What — what would you like?"

"Anything at all, so long as it's made in Kentucky and a hundred proof."

"I'm buyin'!" Angus Mulchay sang out, reaching up to give Buchanan a resounding thump on the back. "But did you never taste real Scot's whisky, lad?"

"Not yet."

"Ah, I wish I had that treat in store. My private bottle," he told Rosemarie grandly, stepping back to survey his guest. "Where'd you come from?" he asked wonderingly.

"No place in particular."

"Is that a fact? And where you bound?"

"Same place."

"You must like it there."

"I like it best wherever I am."

Rosemarie set down the bottle and two tumblers and began to fill them, her eyes never leaving Buchanan's face.

And Hamp Leach was left to stand there, not just ignored by the three of them, but forgotten. To be shamed like this was a brand-new experience, and though he felt a need for some kind of direct action, the gunman plainly didn't know what was expected of him. His Colt was in full view at the end of the bar — no one there had the nerve to touch it — but to walk down and get it was to lose even more face. To take on the sonofabitch bare-fisted was another way, except that he remembered very vividly how the sonofabitch had manhandled him just now.

Rig Gruber came to stand at his elbow.

"Let it lay, Hamp," he advised in a low voice, easing the man aside. "Remember what Gibbons said. We ain't set here yet."

"Let it *lay?* What he did?"

"Just one of them things," Gruber said philosophically. "This ain't your night."

"You wait and see whose night it is. For crissake, look at the raggedy-pants tramp! No gun on him, don't even own boots! Just a goddam, sheepherdin' saddlebum!"

Gruber had noted the same things — the lack of a weapon, the flat-heeled work shoes, the worn clothes and beard stubble.

"But he's been around," Gruber said. "He didn't break his nose or pick up that knife scar herdin' any sheep."

"A friggin' fistfighter," Leach said with all the contempt a gunman has for brawlers. "Riffraff."

"I'd let it lay, Hamp."

"But you're not me, and that's the big difference. Listen — move on down there,

24

casual-like, and get me the Colt."

"You know what Gibbons said . . ."

"Get the Colt, Rig."

For five years Gruber had armied with Leach in one form or another. And from the beginning Leach had bossed him. The habit was hard to break and he moved off now to get the gun.

THREE

Malcolm Lord was still smarting from the tongue-lashing he had received from Angus Mulchay as he sat with his five guests at the round table in the Glasgow's private parlor. He was also apprehensive about the effect of such talk on Captain Gibbons.

"My deepest apologies for the unpleasantness out there, Captain," he said, and it was clear that Lord was not a man called on to apologize very often.

Gibbons waved the subject away.

"I always consider the source, sir," he replied, looking around at the other faces. "I hope you gentlemen have done the same."

The gentlemen returned his gaze levelly and were noncommittal. So far as Messrs. Butler, Watson, Sims and MacPike were concerned this was Malcolm Lord's party. They were his neighbors in the Big Bend, they were here at his invitation, and beyond a vague suspicion about the purpose of this meeting they were content to have it all explained.

But they all had heard the same things about Black Jack Gibbons that Mulchay had spoken outside. As a former officer in the war against Mexico, and captain in the Rangers, the man had spent the last twenty years of his life in the very thick of the never-ending trouble along the vast border. And until a year ago he had been one of the more dashing and admired lesser heroes of the Texas Rebellion, a "typical" Ranger who commanded respect for the badge and the authority by their singular courage, their penchant for enforcing the law almost singlehanded.

A year ago Captain Gibbons had been dispatched to Brownsville to settle a dispute about a beef tally. A group of ranchers insisted that some of their stock had drifted onto the Matamoros range and had been incorporated into Mexican herds. The Mexicans insisted just as stoutly that they had choused the Texas cattle back across the border. What the Texans wanted was free access through Matamoros and the right to inspect the herds for themselves. The Mexicans, feeling that their honor was being challenged and their sovereignty threatened, refused. They would, however, allow the Ranger to come by himself when the

27

roundup was completed and see for himself that there were no American brands present.

His superiors in Austin never got a clear answer from Gibbons as to why he didn't accept this peaceful and reasonable solution. All they knew was that the captain told the Mexicans he would consider the plan, and that during the next six weeks he diligently recruited every ex-cavalryman and jobless rider in the region and formed them into a thoroughly unofficial but quite formidable militia of a hundred expert gunmen. Then, without warning, he hurled that band at Matamoros, and for seventy-two bloody hours they slaughtered all the livestock in sight over a radius of nearly twenty miles.

That was only the beginning. Gibbons led his lawless militia back into Brownsville, where those of Mexican birth exceeded the native Texan population nearly five to one. For ten days the terror lasted — midnight raids, mass trials, mass executions, individual murders — and when it was done there were five hundred less Mexicans in Brownsville.

At his court-martial Gibbons blandly testified that he had uncovered a secret plot to invade Texas: a Mexican army of two thousand was being raised, its arms and men financed by the sale of cattle, most of them stolen from Texas ranches. So he had first struck at the roots of the invasion, killing the herds before they could be marketed. The second part of the plot, according to the accused Ranger, was to be an uprising in Brownsville when the invasion began. "Every Texan," the trial transcript read, "man, woman and child, was to be killed. The only ones to be spared were unmarried women between the ages of fourteen and twenty-one. They were to be transported to Matamoros and handed over to the bandit general, Campos."

So ran Gibbons' defense of his actions around Brownsville. His judges, shocked and disgusted, kicked him out of the service "without honor" and Governor Tatum offered an indemnity of one hundred thousand dollars to the Mexican government. But even with this official condemnation of his act, and the new nickname "Black Jack," there was a large and rather influential number living largely along the border who chose to believe Gibbons' account of his actions at Brownsville and raised their voices in his defense. What the man had done became less and less discussed. It was why he had acted to "save" Brownsville, and they especially admired his saving the flower of

Texas womanhood from the bandit chief.

Opportunity had to knock ever so lightly for Jack Gibbons to heed it. With the support of the more powerful ranchers he made the militia a permanent group, shaving it down to a hand-picked force of fifty gunmen who worked more or less along military lines. For Gibbons had not acted against Matamoros and Brownsville without a long-range plan, an idea calculated not only to make him the kind of controversial figure that satisfied his outsize ego, but also to provide him with a way of life he was born for — to command, to lead men into battle, to create strife and taste victory. All that was in Gibbons, as well as a pathological hatred for the Mexican people.

Malcolm Lord's neighbors had heard many things of the man, and so when he asked them, obliquely, to discount the accusations of Angus Mulchay they were noncommittal. Now, with glasses filled, they turned their attention to their host, the owner of mighty Overlord Ranch.

"Gentlemen," he began gravely, "we are facing a serious problem in the Big Bend and the time has come when those of us with the largest share of responsibility in this country must take steps to solve it."

"Aye," James MacPike said, "the Rio is

low and getting lower. I say wells are our only hope, expensive as they may be . . ."

"I didn't mean the water, MacPike," Lord interrupted testily. "Of course the river's a problem. A big one. Without the river flooding its banks we have no graze."

"What were you referring to, then?" Arthur Butler asked. "What's more important to us than water, Malcolm?"

"Our freedom," Lord told him. "Our heritage. And our duty to our women."

"How's that?"

"The Mexicans," Lord answered. "They cross our border with impunity, come and go on Texas soil just as they please."

"Oh, hell, that's just Angus Mulchay," MacPike said. "He gives the poor devils refuge when the *federales* are nipping too close. Lets them slaughter a few head for fifty dollars."

"And I'll take the overflow," Butler put in. "Damn steady customers, them bandits."

"But you and me ain't on the river, like Angus," MacPike countered. "We all thought the man was daft when he claimed land ten years ago that was a foot underwater. Now look at his fine grass . . ."

The conversation was running away from Malcolm Lord's direction and he cleared

31

his throat impatiently.

"Mulchay is giving comfort to an enemy," he said. "He is helping the bandits survive, strengthening them for an eventual attack . . ."

"Attack?" Thad Sims asked, speaking for the first time.

"Aye, Thaddeus. They have the run of the riverlands now. Some night they'll strike."

"You're living in the past, Malcolm," his friend MacPike objected. "Those raids were ten years ago, and never in the Big Bend . . ."

"And I say that's just what they hope you'll believe. But maybe you'll wish you'd listened to wiser heads, when it's too late and your daughters have been ravaged in their beds!"

"Ah, come down off it!" MacPike said angrily. "Don't be even thinking such a thing, let alone speak it."

"Then heed the man who knows more about our danger than any other. The man I've persuaded to come to our remote range and help us before it's too late." He swung to Gibbons. "Captain, if you please."

"Thank you, sir," Jack Gibbons said, rising from his chair. He held his glass of whisky aloft. "I give you The Lone Star, gentlemen," he said. "A toast to our beloved Texas!"

They drank to that.

"Texas for Texans," Gibbons said then. "I've lived by that creed all my life."

"Are you a native son?" Butler inquired.

"By adoption, sir. I had the misfortune to be born in the state of Georgia. But I came here very young; my daddy saw the opportunity, the destiny. And I fought for the independence of the Lone Star, sir. I remember the Alamo, and called Davy Crockett a friend . . ."

Sacred names were dropping from Gibbons' mouth in profusion, and his listeners were properly reverent.

". . . and I tell you, men, I just wonder what Jim Bowie and Sam Houston would say to us if they could see what we've done with this wonderful country they handed to us."

"Even Mr. Houston couldna kept the Rio high in her banks," MacPike said laconically.

"I'm talking of Mexicans, my friend. We fought them a bitter war, shed our precious blood and won that war. But to the victor belong the spoils? No sir! The government in Austin has let us down. The government in Washington doesn't know we exist. And every God-fearing white man from El Paso to Brownsville is plagued with the enemy he defeated. They squat on his land, raid his herds, cheat good men out of honest labor because they'll work for nothing but their goddam beans and bread.

"I did what I had to do in Brownsville," Gibbons went on, his voice rising dramatically. "This winter I was invited to clean out Laredo, and I cleaned it out. Texas for Texans. Let the brown papists live in their own confines."

"Cleaned out Laredo, you say?" asked Sims. "Exactly what do you mean?"

"Made it safe for a white woman to walk the streets, sir. Drove the troublemakers back across the border where they belong."

"And what do you propose to do for Scotstown?" MacPike asked.

"Mr. Lord has invited me to do the same here," Gibbons said, and Malcolm Lord stood up again.

"Subject, of course, to the approval of us all," the owner of Overlord put in. "What I suggested to Captain Gibbons is that his militia occupy Scotstown for a period of sixty days. The main body of men will patrol the riverlands and rout the Mexicans out when they seek to cross over."

"That could mean fighting."

"It will, James."

"But there's families living there. Mulchay

34

and Bryan, Tompkins, MacKay . . ."

"They'll have to be evacuated."

"Evacuated? Lord, I'd like to see the day when Angus agrees to leave his land."

"This is a common project," Lord said blandly. "If Mulchay is a damned Mexlover, if he gambles with the safety of our children as well as his own, then I say it's up to the community to protect itself. That's the democratic way of it."

"It doesn't sound right, somehow," MacPike said, remembering what Mulchay had been shouting in the saloon — his accusation about Lord trying to steal the land along the riverside. "What," he asked, "does Captain Gibbons get out of it?"

"The opportunity to serve Texas," Gibbons said.

"Aye. But who pays your men and feeds your mounts? Where do you get your guns and ammunition?"

"As I said, sir, Austin has let us down. This war must be financed privately, by patriots."

Thad Sims' head popped up.

"You mean us patriots?" he asked. "We are to pay for this business?"

"A nominal sum," Malcolm Lord assured him. "We'll be assessed according to our holdings."

"That would put the lion's burden on yourself," Sims pointed out.

"There are five of us here," Lord said. "Overlord will underwrite fifty per cent of the expense."

"And what will the total be?"

"Not more than twenty thousand dollars," Gibbons said, and four of his listeners were shocked to the roots of their Scotch-Presbyterianism.

"*Twenty thousand dollars?*" Butler repeated hollowly.

"Fifty men for sixty days," Gibbons said. "And risking their lives every hour of it."

"Fifty crackerjack cavalrymen," Malcolm Lord added. "An elite corps of Texas fighters who'll rid the Big Bend of the Mexican danger . . ."

Arthur Butler was about to put another question to Gibbons, but he never asked it. There was an interruption — the nerve-shattering thunder of gunfire — and it came from just beyond the door.

FOUR

"Well," Angus Mulchay had asked, "how do you like Scot's whisky?"

Buchanan finished his drink and ran his tongue around his lips judiciously. "Not bad," he said. "Not bad."

"Try another," Mulchay said. "Pour, lass."

The girl hesitated.

"I wouldn't go at it too quick," she said to Buchanan direct. "Not the first time."

"Hah!" Mulchay said. "And you're the queen's own taster, are you?"

"I've not tasted the stuff," she said, still not talking to anyone but Buchanan. "But I've sniffed at it once or twice and it's powerful."

"What stuff should I drink?" Buchanan asked.

"They serve a punch up at Armston's," she said.

"Where?"

"The Dance Palace," she told him,

37

smiling. "Oh, it's a lively place . . ."

Mulchay's laughter broke over her voice. "Dancing, she says! For a braehammer the likes of him, with the thirst on him — *dancing!* And sweet lemon punch!"

Buchanan had been called many things in thirty years, but braehammer was a new one. He guessed, though, that it was close to the mark, if not right on it. An outsized, aimless drifter, fit enough company in a saloon but too rough for any social function. He was thinking that and just across the bar the dark-haired girl was smiling at him.

"Pour us a drink," Mulchay said.

"Shall I?" she asked and Buchanan held her steady gaze, then rubbed a palm across a cheek he hadn't shaved in forty-eight hours.

"Yeah," he said. "Fill 'em high."

Hamp Leach had moved back to the door, in quarantine, and his malevolent gaze missed none of the by-play at the bar, the animation in the girl's face, the open flirtation she was carrying on with the no-account who had humiliated him. The contrast between that and the reception he had gotten gnawed on him murderously.

He had the gun back now, riding his hip in its old familiar place. The gun was and always had been the great equalizer between Leach and any other man, and as he looked

38

at the tall figure of Buchanan he fairly itched to feel the butt against his palm, the forefinger triggering humility and death.

Rig Gruber seemed able to read the man's mind.

"Let it lay," he said again.

"Like hell I will."

"What're you gonna do, shoot him in the back?"

"I'll position him, don't worry about that."

"Fill 'em high," Buchanan said. "And pay for them out of this," he added, digging the pouch from his faded denims and tossing it negligently onto the bar.

The girl looked at it and raised her eyes again to his face.

"What is it?" she asked.

"Gold," Buchanan said. "About two ounces' worth, but I'll take your measure."

"My measure for what?"

"Fifty dollars."

Rosemarie laughed at him. "You're fooling," she said. "You're pulling my leg."

"Hold out your hand," Buchanan told her and she laid it meekly inside his huge one. He tipped the pouch and the gleaming, glistening grains of sandlike metal made a conical, two-inch mound in her palm.

Mulchay bent low, eyes wide, and inspected the stuff.

"By God, it is," he said. "Hamlin, MacIntosh — come have a look at this!"

His friends came and had their look, rubbed it expertly between the tips of their fingers.

"Ay," said Hamlin, "it's the McCoy. The root of evil."

"Convinced?" Buchanan asked the girl, but apparently she wasn't.

"Better wait until Mr. Terhune comes in," she said. "I wouldn't dare give you fifty dollars for that — that stuff."

"Then Terhune is standing the drinks," Buchanan told her, wondering if female bartenders were such a good idea after all. "This gold of mine you're holding is all I've got."

"I'll stand you," Rosemarie said and the man named Hamlin cleared his throat.

"No need of that," he said. "I'll buy it from you."

"Sold," Buchanan said.

"Forty dollars," Hamlin said.

Buchanan looked at him. "Fifty," he said.

"Split the difference, laddie. Forty-five."

Buchanan dipped his free hand into the pile inside Rosemarie's palm, pinched an insignificant few grains and scattered them to the floor.

"Now you've got forty-five," he said and

Hamlin nodded, appreciating the fine principle of the transaction. He took a billfold from his pocket and laid out four tens and a five-dollar gold piece.

"Careful now," he cautioned, and Buchanan guided the dust from the girl's hand into the pouch again.

"Where — ah — did you come across the gold?" MacIntosh inquired innocently.

"Won it in a poker game."

"Poker?" Hamlin inquired amiably. "You like the relaxation of the game?"

"That's my roll," Buchanan told him, "less what I owe the lady."

"Then let's have at it," Hamlin said, and six of them proceeded to the nearest table. Cards were produced, everyone anted, and the deal began. Buchanan watched the cards fall, face down, and a grin that was tugging at the corners of his mouth burst full bloom before he picked them up.

"If you've got a new joke," Mulchay said, "let us all hear it."

"No," the big man said, tilting his chair back and looking around at each friendly face with a kind of gratitude on his own. "Just feel real good," he explained.

They all lifted their cards, and under the pretense of studying them, Hamlin stole a long glance at the stranger and was re-

41

minded of a loneliness he had known once.

"How can you play poker without a smoke?" he asked, extending a long cigar across the table.

"Well, thanks," Buchanan said, accepting it. MacIntosh lit it and Buchanan inhaled deeply. Life, he decided, was wonderful.

"Deal me in," a truculent voice ordered and Hamp Leach lowered himself into the last vacant chair, his gaze full on Buchanan's face.

"Next hand," Buchanan said when the dealer seemed not to know the way of it.

"This hand."

Buchanan looked again to the dealer of the game. It was that man's business to set the thing straight, not his, and then he saw all the others had turned to mute statues behind their cards.

"This hand's already been dealt," he said reasonably.

Leach felt the tenseness around the table acutely, the fear, and with a lazy smile he swung his head to the dealer.

"Deal me in," he said and that one gave him five cards. Buchanan debated the rightness of it in his mind, decided that he was having much too good a time, that if they did things that way in Scotstown he was no one to object, and opened the betting with a

42

conservative one dollar.

"Raise you five," Leach said, not even looking at the hand dealt him. Stranger still, he neither had money in front of him nor produced the six he had bet.

The others threw in their hands, quickly, one after the other.

Buchanan cocked an eye at his pair of queens, looked into Leach's unwavering glance and grinned.

"Yours," he said, "and five more," laying his money on the line.

"And five more," Leach said, still not picking up his cards, still not showing any money.

"Cards?" the dealer asked in a small voice and Buchanan asked for three.

"Play these," Leach said.

Buchanan could hardly believe what he had drawn. Another queen and a pair of treys. He suddenly wished that Fargo were standing behind his chair, that his partner could see how many easier ways there were to make money besides mining a Big Bend mountain.

"You opened," Hamp Leach said, "now bet." It was not a reminder but a hard challenge and Buchanan looked at him, at the cards still lying face down on the table, at the prominent gun butt in the cutaway holster, at the unblinking gaze.

"Before you make a play, brother, you better check your hand," he advised him.

"My hand is pat. Bet your own."

"These little darlin's are worth five dollars," Buchanan said affectionately. Mulchay stole a look at the full house and his eyebrows lifted.

"Raise you ten," Leach said.

"All I'm going to do is call," Buchanan told him then. "But first I want to see your money in the middle next to mine."

"I don't need money. I got four queens."

Buchanan laughed. "Only four?" he asked.

"You heard me."

"Added to my three, that makes a strange deck." He put his arm out, turned over Leach's first card. It was a six of hearts.

"Let 'em be," the gunman said, squatting his hand down over the remaining four. "I've got four queens."

Buchanan laid out his full house.

"Now how many do you have?"

"You're calling me a liar?"

Buchanan cocked his head at the man. "Who put the burr in your pants, anyhow?" he asked him.

Leach's chair scraped against the floor and he came out of it threateningly. Now his

44

eyes went to Buchanan's hip, scornfully.

"You think because you're naked," he said, "that you got some kind of protection?"

"Man doesn't need a gun to be right," Buchanan said.

"You're wrong, jasper. You need one bad, and you better go get it."

The words evoked an improbable image in Buchanan's mind, a picture of himself reclimbing the mountain for his gun, coming all the way back down here with it. He smiled.

"What do you think is funny?"

"Nothing tonight, I guess," Buchanan admitted and stood up. He turned his broad back to Leach and started walking away from the table.

"Running, riffraff?" Leach asked harshly. "Had your bluff called?"

Buchanan stopped, looked over his shoulder.

"I'm not running," he told him. "I'm going to borrow a gun."

"No!" Rosemarie protested from behind the bar. "Don't anybody lend him one!"

"Walk out, fella, and keep walking," Angus Mulchay told him shrilly. "You're playing *his* game!"

Buchanan stood before one of the few

armed men at the bar.

"How about yours, friend?"

"Don't give it to him, Mr. White," Rosemarie pleaded. "Don't anyone!"

White shook his head, so did the others.

"He's a gunny on the prod," someone murmured to Buchanan. "Walk away from him like Mulchay says."

"Rig," Hamp Leach called out then. "The riffraff needs your Colt. Give it to him."

Rig Gruber stepped forward, unbuckling his gunbelt.

"Much obliged," Buchanan said, taking it and adjusting the buckle. Then he hefted the .45, checked the fully loaded cylinder. "This your special, mister?" he inquired conversationally.

"Never owned one better."

"With all the weight up front?"

"What's he doin', Rig?" Leach asked loudly. "Tryin' to crawl out?"

"The gun suits me," Gruber said to Buchanan.

"Then I guess it'll have to suit me, too," Buchanan replied. Gruber looked up into his face and an impulse he didn't understand caused him to move directly into Leach's line of fire.

"You don't know what you're in, ranny,"

he said. "That's Hamp Leach."

"Is it?"

"Bodyguard to Black Jack Gibbons."

"Fancy job," Buchanan agreed. "Better get out of the way now." Gruber did, and then Buchanan swung to face Leach. "This fight ain't necessary," he said across the thirty feet that separated them.

"If you're gonna crawl," Leach rasped, "get down on your belly."

"Just pay up your losses and we'll call it square," Buchanan suggested, and it finally got through to Leach that the drifter opposite wasn't begging for an out at all.

"I owe you nothin'," he said. "And no man can call me a liar."

"I do."

"Then draw!"

That was what broke up Malcolm Lord's conference. They heard the shattering explosions but missed the sight of two tall men braced against each other in deadly combat, two hands flashing, two guns exposed and roaring blue-orange flame. All of that in two seconds' time, and with the sound still racketing from the walls and ceiling Hamp Leach sunk to his knees in astonished surprise, and fell dead. It had been a very brief moment of truth for the man, sad in its peculiar way, but no one there was sadder about it than Tom Buchanan.

He carried the borrowed Colt to Rig Gruber, who took it from him automatically, his eyes riveted on the improbable sight of Leach's forever unmoving body.

"Slick shooter, mister," Buchanan told him, "but you ought to lighten the barrel. Doesn't swing up as quick as it might."

"Who's responsible for this?" demanded the authoritative voice of Malcolm Lord then. Buchanan swung to the sound, took in the prosperous-looking group at the doorway.

"If you're the law," he answered Lord, "I guess you mean me."

"I stand for law and order in Scotstown," the rancher said. "What happened here?"

"Thing explains itself," Buchanan said patiently. "Me and him had an argument."

"We all of us saw it, Mr. Lord," the man Hamlin put in. "There was no crime committed."

"Prevention of one," Angus Mulchay announced, surprised that he could speak through his excitement. He whacked Buchanan between the shoulder blades. "Every man in this room owes you a drink, lad, and let Mulchay be the first to treat."

48

"Me next," MacIntosh cried, and from that and the general murmur of approval Malcolm Lord was satisfied that the fight had been conducted according to the standards of the country.

Black Jack Gibbons moved away from the door, knelt briefly beside the dead man, then made a curt signal for Gruber to join him at the quiet end of the bar.

"What did you have to do with this?" Gibbons asked in a fierce undertone.

"Not a damned thing."

"But it was your gun. I saw that much."

"Hamp said give the ranny my Colt. I gave it to him."

"Who is he? What was it all about?"

"A woman," Gruber said. "A poker hand." He shrugged his shoulders. "Hell, in Laredo Hamp plugged a puncher account of the way he wore his hat. He never needed a reason to throw down on somebody."

Gibbons knew all that and more about his bodyguard, but it seemed incredible that he would ever lose his life in a cowtown to a borrowed gun. He stole a glance at the winner, the big man being noisily feted at the other end of the room. If he had ever seen that one before he would remember, and he didn't.

A Ranger? He had been expecting trouble

from Austin ever since Laredo, and it could be their tactics to try to infiltrate the militia, learn their strength and the identity of their riders before moving against him in force.

"Ride out fast to the bivouac," he told Gruber. "Bring back Kersh's squad and tell Lyman to keep everyone else ready to move."

"We working here?"

"They don't know it yet," Gibbons said, "but we are. Get back here quick."

Malcolm Lord was waiting for him when he returned to the private room.

"Where are the rest?" he asked and Lord answered him irritably.

"Gone, Captain," he said. "This shooting incident didn't exactly help our case."

"Are fights so uncommon in Scotstown?"

"Yes, as a matter of fact, they are. Common gunfights, at any rate. I might also point out that your sergeant, or whatever you called him, didn't exactly stand up under your description as an expert with a gun."

The words raked Gibbons' excessive pride in his militia, and color climbed into his cheeks.

"That fellow will have other opportunities

to prove himself," he said.

"How's that?"

"Let it go," Gibbons said, sorry he had spoken. "What about our business?"

"I obviously can't afford your organization by myself. This has been an especially poor year for beef growers."

"But you can subsidize half, as you offered?"

"Yes, I think I can undertake to pay you ten thousand."

"Let's call it settled then, Lord," Gibbons said. "I'll take the other half as I find it."

"I don't think I like the sound of that," Lord told him and the ex-Ranger smiled sardonically at the other man's self-righteousness.

"We each know what we want," he said, "and why we want it. Let's not short-change ourselves by any needless criticism." He picked up the decanter from the table and poured out two tumblers of the mellow liquor. "This is the age of realism, my friend. Let's drink to our mutual understanding."

Malcolm Lord studied the military man thoughtfully, hesitantly, then raised his glass and quaffed it with a single swallow.

"Keep in mind, Captain, that you are a transient. I have to go on living in the Big

Bend when you are gone."

"Who knows?" Gibbons said, a worldly smile touching his lips. "I glimpsed a dark-haired beauty out there who would make the settled life damned attractive. What's the girl's name?"

"Rosemarie," Lord told him. "She's the niece to old Lauren MacKay."

"MacKay? Isn't he one of the river ranchers you mentioned?"

"Aye," Lord said, and there was bitterness in his face. "Six hundred acres of grass growing a foot high. High because the poor impoverished fool doesn't have fifty head of cattle to his name."

"A waste of riches," Gibbons agreed. "You'd think he'd sell."

"Sell? The stubborn old mule won't even lease the graze. But his pride isn't above sending the lass to pour out drinks in a saloon. Puts her to work while he sits on his duff in the shanty he calls a hacienda and prays for a miracle."

"Perhaps the miracle's at hand."

"But not the one he expects," Lord said. "When can your men move onto the land?"

"At any time," Gibbons answered. "They're encamped in the hills and awaiting orders."

"Hold them at the ready," Lord suggested. "I'll have Mulchay's land scouted, and if he's harboring any of his bandit friends your militia can strike."

Gibbons nodded. "I'll take some prisoners," he said, "and march the dirty beggars through town. They leave a good impression, get the right people on our side."

"Then what do you do with them?"

"Try them for their crimes," Gibbons said. "I have a Sergeant Kersh with a knowledge of public trials, and a man named Lyman as interpreter."

"Trial by jury?"

"Always. Gives the town a sense of responsibility. Of course," he added, "I sit as special magistrate."

"But what if Mulchay won't press any charges? Isn't your jury trial likely to prove dangerous?"

"You have not seen Kersh and Lyman try a case against a Mex bandit," Gibbons reassured him. "They do not need the testimony of Mr. Mulchay, believe me."

"I leave it all in your hands," Lord said.

"In a month the riverfront will be evacuated," Gibbons told him. "You can bring your herds in then."

The rancher nodded, and his smile was hard as he shook hands with the ex-Ranger.

"Good night, Captain," he said. "Good luck."

"Luck?" Gibbons echoed. "I make my luck as I go along. And make it for those who go along with me."

Lord left him alone in the room then and Black Jack filled his glass again, sat with it musingly, his mind on many things. He reflected that he was rarely left to himself these days, that the whole tenor of his life had abruptly changed since that assignment to Brownsville, the fateful decision he had made there.

Quo vadis? he asked himself. Well, where *was* he going? How far did his ambition reach? Did Caesar have it all carefully planned when he defied the authorities and crossed the Rubicon? How about little Mr. Napoleon? Had his career been all so crystal clear to him that afternoon *he* took the law into his own hands?

This was not a new subject with Gibbons. Several times he had been reminded of a parallel between what he was doing along the Texas border and what other men had done in their own times. Like them, he had a cause to fight for, a rally-round. "Texas for Texans" meant one thing to Malcolm Lord and another to Hamp Leach — but they both followed where Jack Gibbons led.

Except that Leach was lying dead just beyond this door. Gibbons felt no blame for that, but he did know a responsibility. Just as Caesar would have, had a man outside the ranks triumphed over a trusted centurion. Leach the individual meant nothing — but Leach the handpicked bodyguard for the captain stood for the gun-fighting reputation of the entire militia. Now that reputation had been challenged, besmirched openly.

Gibbons would have liked to do the gallant thing, throw another of his fighters into the arena, and another, and another until the defeat had been wiped from the record. That would have been noble Caesar's way, but Caesar probably didn't have Jack Gibbons' particular problems. For though he had infused a certain *esprit de corps* into his militia they were hardly what a commander would call a dedicated company. What they were were hardcases, the lot of them, and every time he gave an order they first considered what was in it for them. Gibbons thought he had convinced them that the very size of their force was its own best protection, but beyond that simple law of the pack they felt no moral compulsion toward one another. Besides that, it would not strike them as reasonable to take on singlehanded the man who had stopped Hamp Leach.

Still, the fellow had to be handled. Not only because he was living proof that the militia wasn't the best in Texas, but also because of Gibbons' nagging suspicion that he might be a Ranger. And if he had been sent from Austin his handling had to be done in a certain way.

Well, Gruber would be back before long with Kersh's squad, and surely then there'd be enough for the job.

FIVE

Angus Mulchay was one of those outspoken, nimble-witted pepperpots who always either instigated some action or naturally gravitated to the very eye of it. That and his own violent brush with Hamp Leach earlier led him to feel that he had a special companionship with this fellow Buchanan, and convinced him that he had some proprietary interest in the big stranger.

He felt the same about the body of Hamp Leach.

"Leave him lay!" little Mulchay commanded when more sensitive souls went to cover the sprawled corpse with an old horse blanket. "Leave him lay, boys. There's a lesson there for all of us."

"Mr. Mulchay!" Rosemarie scolded.

"There is, lass, there is!"

"And what's the lesson?" Hamlin inquired.

"The Sermon on the Mount," Mulchay recited. "And the meek shall inherit the earth."

His audience heard and ran their eyes over the roughshod Buchanan, remembering the unmeekness in him when Leach had thrown down the gauntlet a few minutes ago. Someone on the fringe of the group laughed.

"And what is humorous?" Mulchay demanded.

"You," the man told him. "But you don't mean to be."

Mulchay was preparing a devastating rejoinder to that when Malcolm Lord appeared from the private room and began making his way out through the saloon proper.

"Well, now," Mulchay said, shifting targets, "did we break up the big secret powwow? I notice you all scurryin' for home soon as the pistols start poppin'."

"Mulchay," Lord said thinly, "I'll thank you to stay out of my affairs."

"Somebody's got to watch you sharp. And where's your new friend, the Brownsville butcher boy?"

"That mouth of yours," Lord said, pausing between the swinging doors, "is going to buy you an early grave. Mark my words!" He was gone then and Mulchay kept staring at the exit somberly.

"Boys," he said at last, "there's trouble

coming to the Big Bend. It'll be hell on horseback if we don't prepare ourselves, and quick."

"You're always seeing trouble, Angus," MacIntosh told him.

"I see what's plain to see. Or do you think Black Jack Gibbons came to pay Scotstown a social call?"

"What did he come for?"

"We'll all find out soon enough," Mulchay predicted, "but by then it'll be too late."

The men's voices sounded all around Buchanan's head like so many droning flies, and held about as much interest to him. He was not geared for town life, had no feeling for it, and as he stood here now looking down into a half-empty whisky glass the big man was asking himself unhappily just what the hell kind of living he was meant for. From the top of the mountain the lights down here had looked warm and inviting, promising a night of companionship with other men. But all that had gone down the trough in sixty seconds, and when Fargo asked him what kind of good time did he have all he could answer was that he had killed a man he'd never even seen before.

He raised his melancholy glance to find the girl watching him from the back bar.

There had been the start of something there, too, he remembered, the possibility of a little harmless dallying that might have been good for both of them. But there was no mischief in her eyes now, no smile tugging at the corners of her lips.

She's got you all pegged out, Buchanan told himself. You couldn't even get the right time from her now.

"Drink up, laddie, and Rosemarie will pour another," Hamlin offered heartily.

He shook his head and stood erect.

"Had enough," he said. He thought, Enough of everything for this night.

"Where you off to?"

"Going to take some air," he said, swinging from the bar.

"But how about your money?" Hamlin protested and Buchanan looked over his shoulder at the currency and coins scattered on the floor.

"Use it to bury him with," he said and walked out of the place, leaving a studied silence in his wake.

"Now there's a type for ye," MacIntosh commented.

"Footloose and fancy-free," Angus Mulchay said. "Just like I was thirty years ago."

"Ay, I saw the resemblance at once,"

60

Hamlin said. "Only you've shrunk a foot since your wild days."

"Size ain't all. You notice I didn't shy from that bully when it was my chance."

"And wound up on the back of your mugg."

"Where d'ye suppose he came from?" MacIntosh asked.

"And where did he come across the gold Hamlin bought?"

"You'll never know, boys," Mulchay said sagely, "and you'll likely never lay eyes on him again. I say we tip the bottle all around and drink one to a gunfighter . . . Rosemarie, what's up, lass?" The girl was retreating along the bar, her head bent low, and Mulchay looked around at his friends. "What's gotten into MacKay's niece?" he asked. "What did I say?"

"Somethin' about us never seein' the fellow again. I don't think that was in the lass's plans for him."

"You mean she's taken with him?"

"From the minute he strolled in."

"With that wildness on him?" Mulchay asked incredulously.

"A moment ago you were drinking his health."

"And will again, for he's a man's man. But he's not what any innocent lass should

61

be fillin' her head with."

"Maybe not," MacIntosh said, "but she's gone off into the black night nevertheless."

Rosemarie fled through the storeroom, her mind in a storm of confusion, and came out onto a dark alley. She found herself next standing in the center of Trail Street, looking in every direction but seeing no sign of Buchanan.

"Mister!" she called plaintively, taking a dozen aimless steps north. "Mister!" Her eyes tried to pierce the darkness, her ears strained for some sound of him. She retraced her steps, went another short distance the other way. "Wait up, mister!" she cried out, feeling even sadder for the very reason she had no name to call him by. She was standing now in the center of Trail Street, a somehow forlorn figure, lost-looking, and made incongruous by the gaily colored bar apron tied at her waist. Beyond her was the familiar front of the Glasgow, beyond that the flickering lights of Armston's Dance Palace. She didn't want to serve drinks any more tonight, and she didn't want to be danced with. In fact, she had a vast number of things she didn't want to do, except be alone, and she started walking toward the river.

A deep voice reached out of the night and caressed her.

"Want any company?" Buchanan asked.

"You! You were there all the while?"

"No, but I wasn't sure which particular mister you were looking for." He came out of the shadows. "Still ain't."

"I know every other name in Scotstown," she explained quietly.

"Tom Buchanan."

"Rosemarie MacKay."

Silence descended over them and they stood looking at each other steadily, seeing only the character outlines of each other's face, and a great many seconds in time passed between them.

At last she spoke.

"Mr. Mulchay said you would not pass this way again."

"No."

"You only came by for a bit of fun, didn't you?"

"Something like that."

"Are you — do you make your way with the gun?" By her hushed hesitancy Buchanan understood that the question went to the roots of her own principles. He also understood that during these past few moments the smoldering fires of his own healthy desires had been stirred, knew for the first time how keen his loneliness had been on that mountain. But some contrariness in the man would not let him compromise her.

"I don't make my way with anything," he told her true. "I'm a bum, a saddlebum —" and then the pixie took hold of him and he laughed. "If I owned a saddle, that is," he added.

And she laughed.

"You mean you ride without a saddle?"

"Without a horse."

"But where do you live?"

A casual twist of his head took in the whole Sierra Negras. "Up there," he said.

"In those fierce mountains? All by yourself?"

"I'm partners with an old gent."

"And you're going back now?"

"Might as well. Got to be there tomorrow anyhow."

"Seems such a lonely life for a — younger man. I mean, sort of wasteful."

"You're telling me it's wasteful," Buchanan agreed with warmth. "All work and no profit."

"I meant, well, physically . . ."

"Yeah, there's wear and tear."

"I'm talking about the years of a person's life," the girl said impatiently. "A man

64

wasn't intended to spend them alone."

"No," Buchanan said, suddenly thoughtful. "I guess not."

"And there's certainly better places to be right here in the Big Bend than on top of that mountain."

"You know something, you got the lonelies tonight yourself."

"Ay."

"Well, then, let's do something together."

"Oh, yes! Do you like to dance?"

"Till the cows come home."

"Then it's off to Armston's," she said, linking her arm through his and leading him back toward the dancehall.

"Fine night, isn't it?" he asked her.

"Fine and dandy," she assured him. "I have the feeling that anything could happen on a night like this."

SIX

They wheeled into Trail Street, seven of them riding abreast of each other, and a bystander marked the arrogance of that, the seizure of the right-of-way. He also noted the armament — not only revolvers but rifles in their saddles — not he watched them pass before he went his own way, uneasier than he had been a moment before.

Rig Gruber signaled the party to a halt some fifty feet before the Glasgow.

"Just you and me better go in to see Gibbons," he told Lou Kersh. "The rest of you spread yourselves in front of the place and wait."

"I could use a drink, Rig," one of them complained.

"That's just what Hamp said, Mac, and Hamp ain't with us no more."

Mac spit into the dust to show what he thought of that. But he held his seat while Gruber and Kersh dismounted, hitched reins to the rail and entered the saloon.

"So you're back," Angus Mulchay said, the official greeter. "And brought another bully-boy to test the champion."

The cold eyes of both gunmen studied him impassively, taking his measure. But whatever decision they came to was their own secret as they passed on toward the closed door without speaking. While Gruber knocked, Lou Kersh directed the same impersonal glance at the sprawled figure of Hamp Leach. The door opened a crack, then Gibbons pulled it ajar and let them inside.

"Where'd he go, Cap?" Gruber asked.

"He's not at the bar?"

"No."

"Did you pass anybody coming in?"

"Couple of families in wagons. No single rider his size."

"Then he's still around," Gibbons said. "Let's go look him up."

"One question," Kersh said. "What's so important about him, whoever he is?"

"Whoever he is," Gibbons answered, "he shot and killed a militiaman on duty."

Kersh was unimpressed by the armylike jargon.

"Hamp drew, didn't he?" he asked dryly.

"You're missing the point," Gibbons told him, his own voice testy. "We're an organization, all of us together, and what happens to one happens to all. Our reputation in this town and every other town depends on how we take care of our own men. Is that clear, mister?"

"It'd be clearer," Kersh said, "if it were anybody but Hamp Leach."

"Personalities don't enter into it. But if you still need a reason to take this ranny, let me tell you that I think he could be from Austin."

"That's a lot different," Kersh agreed. "Been expecting some trouble like that since we hit Laredo."

"And this is the only way they could handle it. Most people don't realize it, but at fifty strong we're more than twice the size of all the Rangers put together."

"So they send one at a time."

Gibbons nodded. "And he's supposed to take as many of us as he can."

Kersh smiled cynically. "Hard work for poor wages," he said. "Even the boys at Alamo got better odds than that."

"And no boys have it better than Gibbons' militia," Gibbons told him. "Don't you forget it, Kersh."

"No complaints, Captain."

"Then let's flush this bird of ours." Gibbons opened the door and the three of them passed through into the saloon. Abruptly, Gibbons stopped. "For God's sake," he snapped at the remaining bartender, "are you going to leave this man's body here the whole night?" But the bartender shrugged his round shoulders. He only worked here, the gesture said; when Mr. Terhune got back, speak to him about it.

"We bury our own dead, Black Jack Gibbons," Mulchay said then.

"And you might be talking your way into a grave, old man," Gibbons told him, then switched his attention to Hamlin. "Isn't there an undertaker in town?" he asked.

"Simmons does a nice funeral," Hamlin answered civilly. "None of your fancy caskets and all, but he gets them under the ground in fine style."

"And where is Simmons?"

"Bein' Saturday, he's up the street, playin' the fiddle and callin' the reel."

Gibbons took a twenty-dollar gold note from his vest, carried it to the bar. "Send for him," he told the bartender. "Tell him I want Sergeant Leach laid out in military fashion."

"It's all bought and paid for," Mulchay said.

"By whom?"

"By the same lad that so calmly plugged

your sergeant, and him with a borrowed weapon . . ."

Gibbons' hand came down on the bartop hard. "As you just explained," he said angrily, "we bury our own dead." With that he strode from the place, Gruber and Kersh at his heels.

Angus Mulchay followed, showing none of the temperate caution of his neighbors. So far as they were concerned, Gibbons and his gunmen could come and go with no interference from them. Especially they could go. Mulchay was back within sixty seconds, his face alive with concern.

"There's a gang of them — a whole dirty gang of them!" he said, outraged.

"Have a wee knock, Angus," Hamlin advised, "and be thankful they're not out there on your account."

"Ay," Mulchay retorted, "it's the lad's turn tonight. Tomorrow it's me, then you. And next, you, MacIntosh . . ."

"Don't talk daft, man. What harm have I done the likes of Black Jack Gibbons?"

"You made the mistake of settlin' riverland that the almighty Malcolm Lord wants. You stood with me and MacKay and wouldn't sell out."

"And still won't. But what's that to do with anything?"

"Lord brought Gibbons to Scotstown, right?"

MacIntosh nodded.

"And Gibbons don't roam the border for his health, right?"

"So it's said."

"Said? Man, I was there not two weeks after the massacre. I saw the graves with me own eyes."

"We know, we know," Hamlin told him.

"Then know something else," Mulchay said. "Lord and Gibbons are going to make a grab at our holdings."

"My title is clear," MacIntosh protested. "I'll have the law on them!"

Mulchay laughed in his friend's face.

"By law do you mean Bart Taggart, him so stiff with the misery he cannot even walk the length of Trail Street? Or the deputy, him more interested in dancin' Saturday night than whatever befalls?"

"The law in Austin, then," MacIntosh said, suddenly less confident. "I'll have a Ranger down here to protect my rights."

"Better hitch up your buggy right quick then," Mulchay said. "You'll be there in a week. Maybe they'll even send two Rangers back with you — two against Gibbons' cutthroat army."

They were soberer men now than they

had been two minutes ago.

"What is it you suggest, Angus?"

"That we do now what we would have done in '37. Defend ourselves, man!"

"But this isn't '37. Why, I haven't even bought one of those new rifles . . ."

"We'll fight them with anything we can lay hands on," Mulchay told him. "Knives and clubs, rocks — anything."

"But Gibbons is all proper military, so they tell me. Cavalry and the like, and every man a veteran of hard combat."

"There's one," Mulchay said, pointing to Leach. "Personal bodyguard to the great poobah himself."

"But it took the lad to lay him out. Most likely a gunfighter in his own right."

"What's your alternative, then — just roll over and play dead?"

"Ah, you're just making wild guesses," Hamlin told him. "You're worse at ringing false alarms than the boy in the meadow."

"Good night to ye," Mulchay said, turning his glass face-down on the bar, the classic, old-country symbol that his night's drinking was ended.

"Where you going?" his friend asked, much concerned.

"Where Mulchay goes and what Mulchay does," he shouted at them, "is from now on

Mulchay's business!" Something caught the fiery Scotchman's eye and he changed direction to cross toward Leach. He bent down over the dead man, rolled him over as he would a sack of meal and exposed the ex-gunman's once-fired .45. He picked up the weapon and jammed it deep into the pocket of his worn coat.

"Angus!" Hamlin cried. "Ye can't go up against the lot of them. Not single-handed!"

"The gun's for the laddie-buck," Mulchay said. "This is his fighting chance — and may it prove luckier for him than the last man that owned it." With that he left the Glasgow.

"Try that place first," Gibbons said, indicating the noisy, brilliantly lit Armston's dancehall. He had not missed the added absence of the shapely bargirl from the saloon and now was guessing that she might have taken up with their quarry for a bit of Saturday night-life in Scotstown. The five mounted men were afoot by this time and they formed a sort of phalanx with the other three; a tight, troublesome-looking group of eight.

"Do we take him on sight, or what?" Rig Gruber asked when they were at the foot of the dancehall steps.

"You're entitled to the first crack," Gibbons said.

"How come?"

"He shot Leach with your gun, didn't he?"

"But this gun don't swing just right," Gruber said. "Too much barrel."

"It worked all right for him."

"Man's got those long arms," Gruber argued. "Makes all the difference."

"Swing mine," his buddy Kersh offered.

"Swing your friggin' own."

"Who we bucking, anyhow?" Kersh asked. "Another Texan Thompson?"

"Go on in and find out," Gruber suggested.

"What's gotten into you?" Gibbons demanded angrily. "I was sure you'd jump at the chance."

"Thanks all the same, Cap'n, but I pass."

"Then he's yours, Kersh," Gibbons said, but Kersh shook his head.

"I'll brace anything that walks," he said, "if I have to. But since we all got stakes here why don't we all take him? Then adjourn to the oasis next door and pull the cork."

They were thinking very much of Hamp Leach, Gibbons knew, remembering that Leach had the rep. And the ex-Ranger was learning, too, that for a situation such as this he had done his work on them too well. Gruber and Kersh had grown accustomed to the Army way, fighting as a group, and their individuality was gone.

"We're waiting on you, Cap," Kersh said, but the words had a different meaning for Gibbons. They were waiting on him and his mind traveled back one year. He saw himself a Ranger again, imagined the man inside the dancehall a wanted criminal. He wouldn't have hesitated two seconds.

"What's it gonna be, Cap?" Kersh asked.

"Let's go," Gibbons said. "We'll take him together," and he started up the steps first, telling himself that he could still do that, at least. A year hadn't changed him *that* much.

"... *now doe-see-doe to the left and right — and swing your gal with all your might!*"

Buchanan took the fiddler at his word, swung Rosemarie clear off the floor, round and round, effortlessly, and the girl squealed in pretended dismay as her petticoats ballooned above her shapely knees.

"... *now promenade past all your friends . . . salute your partner as this dance ends!*"

The amiable giant made a sweeping bow to the curtseying beauty and when their glances met an infectious smile passed between them.

"Never danced with a grizzly before, did you?" he asked as they walked off the floor.

"Why, you're as graceful as could be," she protested, and then lowered her voice confidentially. "Only not so vigorous with the swinging, Tom. I'm sure I shocked all the ladies present."

"And pleased all the gents, which brings you out even."

"Evenin', Miss MacKay," interrupted a puncher of Buchanan's own age, but clean-shaven, togged out in a bright new shirt and reeking of bay rum.

"Evening, Billy," Rosemarie answered. "I'd like you to meet Mr. Buchanan. Tom, this is Billy Neale."

"Howdy."

"Howdy."

The men shook hands and Buchanan stood by patiently until Neale had gone over him from shaggy head to scuffed work shoes. Neale switched his attention to the girl.

"Thought you had to work tonight, Rosemarie?" he said pointedly.

"I'm playing truant," she confessed. "I should be at the Glasgow now."

"Apparently you're more persuasive than I am," Neale said to Buchanan.

"No," Rosemarie answered for him. "It

76

was I who did the persuading."

Neale didn't take that explanation very well at all.

"Live in the Big Bend, Buchanan?" he asked.

"Nope. Just dropped down for a couple hours."

"Dropped down? From where?"

"The mountains," Buchanan told him vaguely. "Fact is," he said, turning to Rosemarie, "I better be starting back."

"Oh, no! There're still a lot more dances."

"My partner'll be looking for me bright and early."

"But we're having such a good time! You mustn't leave now."

"What are you doing in the mountains?" Neale asked, more nettled-sounding each time he spoke.

"Living by the skin of my teeth."

"So it looks. They tell me there's supposed to be gold up there."

"I wouldn't say that —"

"Psst! Laddie!" a sharp voice beckoned. "Big fella — over here!"

Buchanan swung to see Angus Mulchay motioning to him excitedly from a side door.

"What is it, Tom?" Rosemarie asked anxiously.

"Don't know," he said and went to the old man.

"Clear out while you can, son. Black Jack Gibbons is coming in the front door with a gang of 'em."

"Gang of what?"

"Murderers — and you're their meat if they corner you in this box!"

"Oh, Tom — look!" Rosemarie cried at his shoulder and Buchanan saw eight men with guns already drawn, eight pairs of eyes scanning the room. A woman spotted them and uttered a piercing scream. The fiddler's bow stopped in mid-note, dismayingly, and then all was quiet.

"Run for it, Tom!" Rosemarie urged him. "They haven't seen you yet."

"Hell, they wouldn't shoot . . ."

"You're wrong, man, wrong!" Mulchay told him. "You're no more to that crew than a stray dog. Take this," he said, passing over the gun, "and make a break —"

"Over there!" Rig Gruber shouted. "By the door!"

"Move away from him, girl!" Jack Gibbons commanded in a strong voice. "You, too, old man, unless you want to die beside him!"

"Hold it, mister," Buchanan called to him. "Whatever this quarrel's about, let's get it outside."

"We like you just as you stand," Gibbons answered harshly. "Just move out from behind those skirts!"

"No!" Rosemarie cried, throwing her arms around Buchanan. "No!" she cried again, defiantly.

Gruber had been sighting the shot for ten seconds. Now he triggered it, and with the roaring crash of the six-gun Buchanan felt a jarring blow at his collarbone, a searing pain. He spun the girl out of the fire line, not gently, and with anger sparking every new move, he wheeled and drove three slugs into the crouching Gruber — fatal punishment for the cynical chance the gunman had taken with Rosemarie's innocent life.

"Watch the girl!" Gibbons was shouting above the awful melee, and Kersh and the man beside him opened fire heedlessly. Something burned into the flesh of Buchanan's thigh and his right arm was suddenly turning numb.

"Run for it, man, run!" Angus Mulchay pleaded. "This way —" and Buchanan turned his broad back to the fight, made it through the doorway and staggered out into the night like some drunk. The door was slammed shut behind him and then it was very dark in the alley.

"Can ye move, lad?" Mulchay asked at his

side. "Can ye make it to Ferguson's house?"

"Take care of yourself, friend. Those sons of bitches hold life damn cheap."

"I'm next, anyhow, so follow me now if ye can!"

It was such a frustrating thing. His mind was clear — purged by the rage that was whipping it — and his eyes made out the slender little man moving ahead of him. But nothing else responded to his will. From the shoulders down, his whole body was sluggish, tiredly disobedient — and with no warning at all his bleeding right leg buckled beneath him.

"Get up, boy! Try! Can't ye hear them coming around the front?"

Buchanan used the side of the wall to regain his feet again, used it once more to make his way forward.

"He's in there!" shouted a voice that was becoming raggedly familiar. "This time," Gibbons ordered, "get him!"

Buchanan shifted the gun to his left hand, pumped two roaring welcomes into the alley's narrow mouth, heard two anguished groans. But Buchanan took little heart from that, for he had pulled the trigger three times — there was no more argument left in Hamp Leach's Colt.

Mulchay was supporting him and pulling

him at the same time, his eyes closed, body rigid as he waited for the sniping bullet with his name on it. But Buchanan's last volley had written caution into the hearts of Gibbons & Co. and they answered it with snap shots, an uneven fusillade that passed high and wide of the two fugitives. At last they came to a door in the side of a house — only sixty feet from where they had started the journey, but an eternity in time — and Mulchay turned the knob in his hand.

"We're forsaken, son," he moaned. "Ferguson's is locked against us."

Buchanan didn't have much left, but he gave it all in a grunting lunge against the jamb. The wood splintered and the lock sprung, the door flew open and Buchanan went on inside with it.

"Be damned and you're the man for me!" little Angus congratulated him. "But ye got to get up, son. They're not likely to stay put out there for long."

"You go ahead, dad," Buchanan told him peacefully. "I think I'll wait for them here."

"If you wait, I wait," Mulchay said definitely. "We'll go out together."

Buchanan made no sense out of that, so he made the struggle to stand another time. Helpful old coot, but loco, he thought irrelevantly. Wonder if he knows Fargo?

"You know Fargo?"

"Town in the Dakotas. What about it?"

"This is a fella. Funny little guy. Talked me into busting my back against a goddam mountain."

"Godsakes, lad, this is no time for pleasant memories! If we're going, we got to get!" The house was darkened, vacant because Ferguson and his family were visiting, but Mulchay led Buchanan through it familiarly. They crossed the kitchen, the parlor, started up a flight of steps.

"I'm leaking blood all over the carpet," Buchanan said.

"I'll pay Andy Ferguson for all damages. Oh, Harry — here they come again!"

Gibbons had convinced his warriors that the alley was safe by venturing into it himself, and now they were at the sprung door, noisily cautious.

"Kersh, you and Mills get around to the front. Boland and Milton follow me in here. Everybody ready?"

Angus and his big friend were on the landing by this time, but the words of Gibbons came to them loud and clear, taunting them.

"I've got another plan," Angus whispered desperately.

"Anything you say," Buchanan answered,

feeling lightheaded from the loss of blood.

"Stop Black Jack and we've stopped 'em all."

"Sure."

"He's got the milk-colored Stetson," Mulchay murmured. "Do you think you can spot him when he climbs up the stairs?"

"Sure."

"Then shoot straight and true. It's the best chance we have."

"Can't."

"What?"

"Can't shoot. No more ammo. Left the gun downstairs."

"Good grief!"

"Here's a gun on the floor, Cap!" shouted a voice below, a triumphant echo to Mulchay's melancholy voice. "Empty! He's all shot out!"

Gibbons' burst of laughter betrayed his relief. Four of his best had gone today — he would sorely miss the Leach-Gruber team — and his thoughts on entering this blacked-out house had been that if he didn't lead the attack up those stairs, no one would. What an un-Caesar-like end that would have been for Jack Gibbons — death from a stranger in another stranger's home. But the Lady called Luck hadn't deserted him yet.

"He's all mine," Gibbons said quietly, moving with confidence to the staircase, starting to mount the steps.

Mulchay tugged Buchanan along the upper corridor and led him into a kind of storeroom in a makeshift attic. He went to the single window, unclasped the shutters and pushed them outward.

"Can ye get your good leg over the sill?" he asked. "There's a thin cornice and a sloped roof."

"We both can't make it," Buchanan said in a weakening voice. "Go on, and good luck."

"If it's as far as you can go," Mulchay announced, "it's as far as I can go." They both could hear the steady fall of Gibbons' boot heels ascending the stairs.

"Well, so long," Mulchay said, "whatever your name is."

"Buchanan."

"My pleasure, lad, to know ye briefly and to go out of this life by your side."

"The window," Buchanan said wearily, feeling that he was being blackmailed into moving. "Let's go."

He went through the opening somehow, somehow steadied both legs on the ten-inch cornice while he leaned against the shingled roof and edged slowly toward the outline of the building next to this one. Angus got out there, too, and quietly reclosed the shutters.

The old man began inching his way along, not daring to look down at the street below. He knew without looking that there were two men guarding the front door, a scant twenty feet down, and the slightest sound that attracted their attention up here signed his death warrant.

Then his foot dislodged a pebble, and he choked back a gasp as the small stone rolled over the cornice. Mulchay heard it strike the wooden sidewalk and bounce. A long, long second went by. Another. But there was no roar from a gun, no bone-shattering bullet — and Mulchay found he was almost bursting his lungs from the breath he still held.

He resumed following Buchanan, inches at a time. The building adjoining Ferguson's house was Smith's hardware store, some four feet lower than the home, but flat-roofed. Buchanan lowered himself to it and helped Mulchay down.

"Pray for us now," Angus whispered, moving to a metal door that was set into the roof itself. "Pray that my friend Tom Smith is a careless man." He bent down, grabbed the handle and tugged at it. The door held fast.

"He's not careless," Mulchay said, defeated.

Buchanan pulled at the stout handle, hard, but the iron bolt on the other side yielded not at all.

"Now what?" he asked.

"Now we've had it," Angus told him. "There's no other way down from here."

It seemed to Rosemarie MacKay that terror was piled upon terror. Buchanan was gone, but she could still see his blood-soaked shoulder, the wound in his leg, felt herself being flung away from him and out of danger. He had fled to safety himself, but his attackers, like wild dogs, charged to the pursuit.

"Rosemarie, are you all right?" Billy Neale asked her anxiously. "Were you hit?"

"We've got to help him!" the girl cried. "Somebody has to help!"

"Who is the fellow? What's he wanted for?"

"He fought a bully in the Glasgow. Shot him fair . . ."

"But aren't they law officers?" Neale asked, incredulous.

"No! They're hired killers, and the one in charge was brought here by your own boss!"

Neale shook his head. "Mr. Lord has no need for gunmen," the cowboy said loyally.

"Why, he's a town councilman."

"I know what I see and what I hear," Rosemarie told him. And then the firing commenced again in the alley. "They've found him! Oh, God, won't somebody help?" And she would have run out there herself if Neale and another man hadn't held her fast.

"What can you do?" Neale shouted at her. "What can anyone do? None of us come here armed, not even the deputy."

"Let me go," she demanded. "Let me go! He has to have somebody!"

But Neale moved her toward the front of the hall, away from the sound of gunfire. The crowd in here was of three minds. One group clustered around the body of Rig Gruber, while Deputy Crane — a white-faced, shocked-looking young man — searched in vain for some sign of life. Another bunch huddled along the farthest wall, asking each other what had happened. A third had started to stream out of the place, then quickly came back inside when the shooting recommenced.

"Please take me out of here," Rosemarie pleaded, too spent to resist the firm hold he had on her. "Please."

That, in fact, struck the cowboy as not a bad idea. If they had him cornered in the alley the fellow might very well duck back in here again. So he led the distraught girl out onto the street, unaware that at the same moment Buchanan and Mulchay were working their way to Ferguson's across the alley. Now there was a pause in the firing, but the voice of the man in the white hat came to them.

"He's in there," it said. "This time, get him!"

"He's still alive, then!" Rosemarie cried hopefully. "There's still a chance for him!"

Neale hustled her quickly across the street, but when he would have moved her to even further safety she struggled against him.

"No, no! I won't leave. There's still a chance!"

"A chance for what? What can you do for him?"

"I don't know. I just don't know . . ." Her voice broke off at the sight of two gunmen emerging from the alley.

"What are they doing, Billy?"

"Sealing off the front of the house," Neale told her.

"It's so uneven — all of them, and all he did was defend himself against that troublemaker."

Her words stirred an uneasiness in Neale's mind. He saw now that his first conclusion — that they were lawmen hunting a desperado — didn't stand up. Not only had Buchanan been plainly unarmed when he arrived at the dance, but no peace officer in Texas would have fired at him across the floor with Rosemarie obscuring his shot. But wanting to help was one thing. Actually helping was another. Gunplay — even if he had a weapon with him — was foreign to Billy Neale's character. He was born and raised for nothing else but ranching, the peaceable, workaday life of raising cattle and sending them to market. He owned a Colt's repeater, but damned if he could hit anything with it beyond ten feet. That was what shocked him about the shot fired so close to the girl, and amazed him that the Buchanan fellow could have returned it so unerringly.

"There's a shotgun behind the bar at the Glasgow," Rosemarie said, as if reading his mind. "Run and get it, Billy."

"You come with me."

"No. I've got to stay here. It's — I've just *got* to."

The cowboy went off to the saloon, not understanding the female mind, the fundamental need to keep a vigil, the belief that her personal presence lent weight to the prayer she offered up.

And hardly had Neale left her side but the girl saw the shutter open in the upstairs window. Then, with her heart beating triphammer blows against her breast, Buchanan appeared there and proceeded to step out on the decorative cornice. She noticed at once how woodenly he moved, like a man walking in his sleep, and she was certain that with his next step he would lose his balance and fall to the street.

That dire thought reminded her of the two gunmen directly below. *They must not look up. If they did . . .*

Now Mr. Mulchay was out of the window, closing the shutters, leaning awkwardly against the slanted roof and edging along. Something made the man suddenly stop and she saw his small body freeze with terrible anticipation. What caused it she could not tell.

For twenty seconds she stood there and watched the two of them cross. Twenty years. Twenty eons. But then Buchanan was stepping down to the roof of Smith's store, and Mr. Mulchay made it. Not out of danger yet, not nearly, but worlds safer than they had been from the moment the gunmen had entered the dancehall.

What now? she wondered. In back of the hardware store was a small yard, beyond that the lumber yard and Donhegan's stable. The stable! Horses!

Almost without realizing it, the girl was crossing the street, taking a diagonal route that would precede Buchanan to Donhegan's. The practical thought was to prepare a mount for him, have it saddled and ready to fly. In the back of her mind was a wild notion — to make two horses ready and ride away with him.

A violent movement up above made her look to the Ferguson window. The man called Gibbons had slammed the shutters open and was glancing all around.

"Kersh! Didn't you see him?"

"Hell, no."

"Damn it, he must have gone this way! Passed right over you!" With that, Gibbons stepped out onto the ledge and started moving purposefully in the same direction his quarry had.

SEVEN

"Ye hear what I hear?" Angus asked. The little man had been walking around, restless as a bird. The big one was stretched out below him, the thumb of his left hand plugged into the hole the bullet had made. It was surprisingly effective in staunching the outgo of his life's blood.

"Did ye hear?" Mulchay asked again.

Buchanan nodded. "Always that same damn voice."

"We'll be hearing more than his voice in another minute."

"Not you, oldtimer."

"The hell ye say! It's two birds with one stone tonight for Black Jack Gibbons."

"What did you ever do to him?"

"Claimed bottomland when the Rio was at high flood, that's what."

"Can't shoot you for that."

"Can if it benefits Malcolm Lord — can, and will!"

"Well, in case it doesn't," Buchanan said

— obviously not believing that anyone would kill old Mulchay — "in case it doesn't I want to will you my goods."

"We're goin' out together, lad! That's a fact."

"Consistin' just about entirely of a one-half claim in the Lucky Monday Mine —"

"Will ye quit jabberin'? It's Last Saturday for the both of us!"

". . . can't give you any positive location, except it's in the Negras and you take the trail west by two peaks of Big Chisos. Then just keep climbin' until somebody takes a potshot at you. That'll be Fargo, but he can't shoot worth a Mex dollar."

"Here he comes!" Mulchay said, dropping to one knee. "Ah, lad, if ye had your health. If ye had a gun . . ."

Gibbons stepped cautiously to the flat roof of the hardware store, stood there waiting until he was joined there by the two he had detailed to follow him.

"Can you see them?"

"Black as tar pitch, Cap'n. You sure he ain't armed?"

"Positive."

"But he'll have a knife. Don't want a gutful of that."

Gibbons hadn't considered a blade. As a Ranger he'd never carried one, figured it as

93

Mexican. But Texas Thompson had, one Jim Bowie had made for him, and so had others who worked the border.

"We'll each take a corner," Gibbons said, his bravado tempered. "Work toward the center, and keep talking. Anything else that moves, shoot it." They went where he told them to go. "Start," he commanded and all three began converging toward the door in the middle of the roof.

Buchanan and Mulchay had heard it all.

"Ye don't, do ye?" Angus whispered.

"No knife," Buchanan answered, and that was that. Each man lapsed into silence, thinking his own thoughts, but the will to live was still with them, for the silence was absolute and their assassins would get no help in their work.

Buchanan gave his personal attention to Gibbons, gauging the direction he would come from, listening closely to each footfall. When he thought it was time he pulled his thumb from the wound and flexed all the fingers of that good hand. His last request wasn't outlandish — only the chance to use that hand on Gibbons to leave the man something to remember him by.

They were both listening so hard to death that neither heard the bolt being slid back from the door. Then the door moved beneath Mulchay's arm and the old man shouted out loud.

Three guns exploded a startled, fearsome reply, thundered another time, again — and nine murderous slugs crisscrossed all about the heads and legs of the two prone men, so close they could smell them and all but taste the scorching lead.

And in the midst of everything that was happening, Buchanan marveled at the single-minded courage of whoever it was who kept pushing that door wider.

"Down here, down here," Mulchay was yelling at him, and then Mulchay was abruptly gone, pulled to safety by an unseen hand. Buchanan crawled into the dark opening, was also tugged head first down the stairway. The heavy door slammed closed above him.

"Good work, Billy," said a voice he recognized as Hamlin's, from the saloon. "That took sand."

Second the motion, Buchanan tried to say, but the effort just to speak seemed too much now. Very quietly the big man passed into unconsciousness.

EIGHT

There was no truce in the private war between Gibbons' Militia and Tom Buchanan
— only a ceasefire, and that arranged by
Malcolm Lord.

It was done by an ultimatum, delivered
sternly.

"Have you taken leave of your senses,
Captain?" the rancher demanded, his voice
outraged.

"Lower your voice, sir," Gibbons retorted, his own temper on a very short fuse.
"This is a question of principle. I'll brook
no interference."

"All right, then! Keep after that fellow in
there, whoever he is! I'm told you've already
wounded him badly, but keep on with the
hunt, Captain — and when you've finally
killed him take your fine militia out of
Scotstown and keep it out!"

"We have an arrangement, Lord . . ."

"*Had!* Do you think I could possibly go
through with any proposition if you con-

tinue? I brought you here to clear the country of hostile Mexicans. My motives are valid. But, great God, do you think I can sponsor your troops if this is how they work? Either withdraw from this sorry affair immediately or go your way alone."

Rarely did Black Jack Gibbons decline a challenge, or swallow an angry reply, but he did so now — and for a very practical reason. Unknown to Malcolm Lord, Gibbons' Militia was in perilous financial condition. Its commander had ample funds and a few lucky camp gamblers, but some forty-odd men hadn't been paid in a month, and the monthly payroll was a sizable four thousand dollars. Nor, if he should lose this "commission" in the Big Bend, would he be able to meet next month's payroll. Gibbons needed Lord's ten thousand very badly — and whatever else he could get his hands on.

So he called off the siege of Smith's hardware store, but not without some face-saving. With Malcolm Lord and Doc Church as intermediaries, Gibbons had himself escorted inside the store and into the backroom where Buchanan had been carried. There, besides the unconscious man, and Mulchay, he found Rosemarie MacKay, Billy Neale, Hamlin, MacIntosh, and Smith himself.

"Give up, have ye, Black Jack?" asked the belligerent little Angus. "Or are ye just stallin' for time?"

"Be quiet, Mulchay!" Lord told him. "The captain has something he wants to say."

"I'll be brief," Gibbons said, shifting his steady glance from the face and figure of the girl to include them all. "You've seen fit to give aid and comfort to an enemy of mine. In this instance — since you in the Big Bend aren't fully aware of the important services my men are rendering the great state of Texas, the sacrifices they are making to protect your women, your children and your property from the ravaging Mexican bands — in this instance I'll overlook the matter and take no reprisal.

"As for him," Gibbons went on, looking to the bloody figure on the cot, "I can grant no such amnesty."

"Ye mean ye'd still kill the lad?" Mulchay demanded.

"I give him safe conduct out of Scotstown," Gibbons said. "It expires in twenty-four hours, at midnight tomorrow — and from one minute past midnight he'll be killed on sight."

With that Gibbons swung on his heel and stalked out. Lord followed Doc Church to

98

where Buchanan lay, looked on as the medico listened for a heartbeat.

"Rough-looking customer you got there, Doc," the rancher said, frowning. "Wouldn't want to meet him in the dark."

"Don't say such a thing," Rosemarie protested with heat. "He's as gentle as a kitten."

"Killed two and wounded two," Lord said. "And hasn't been in town three hours."

"And arrived unarmed, Malcolm Lord," Mulchay put in. "Looking for a sociable drink and a little poker — until your friend the butcher turned his dogs loose on him."

Lord paid no attention to him. "I'd advise you all," he said, "and especially you, young lady, to get shut of this fellow immediately. He's bad medicine, mark my words . . ."

"Beats me," Doc Church said, breaking in. "This horse's heart is hammering away like he was no more than sleeping real heavy. Somebody get me some rags and a pan of water." Rosemarie hurried off and the doctor turned to the owner of the store. "Left my bag at home, Tom — mind if I borrow what I need?"

"Don't stock doctor's things, but help yourself."

Church wandered into the store proper,

returned with a paring knife, a thin chisel and long-jawed pliers. Rosemarie returned with the water and pieces she had stripped from her petticoat.

"Billy," Church said then, "he may come to with a roar. Think you can hold him down?"

"I'll sure try."

"And if Billy can't hold him, will somebody else stand by to conk him out again?"

"I'll do that," Mulchay volunteered. "The laddie can trust me to bash him gently."

Church bent to his work without further ado, and Malcolm Lord, feeling suddenly in need of air, went out of the place. Under the pain of the probing knife, then the chisel, Buchanan began to stir. Church worked the slug loose, and Buchanan groaned deep in his chest. The pliers went into the wound, got purchase on the lead bullet, and when Church yanked it free Buchanan rose to a wide-eyed sitting position. He roared, as the doctor had predicted, and his left hand clamped around the doctor's windpipe — all in the pure instinct of self-preservation. But Church was in great danger of being strangled, what with Mulchay's blows with the ax handle only convincing Buchanan's brain that it was fighting for life. It was

Rosemarie, yanking the handle from Angus's fingers, who supplied the anesthesia. Buchanan's body went limp and his chin fell against his bare chest.

"Well, thank you," Church said when he could speak again. "That boy can grab hold good." He was surprised to see the girl break out into tears, and with a shrug he went about blocking the fresh spurt of blood and bandaging the wound. He gave the thigh his attention then, stripping the trouser leg away, and made the happy discovery that the bullet had forced its own way out of the flesh. "Look at the leg on the fellow, would you?" he asked admiringly. "I tell you, boys, that is sinew. Make awful tough eating, this horse."

"Damn it, Doc," MacIntosh said, "there's a female present. And an unmarried one, to boot."

"It is a manly leg," Rosemarie said, brushing the tears from her eyes. "And nothing to cause me embarrassment, married or no."

"Not very fond of my patient, are you?" Church teased.

"No, not very."

"Figure to nurse him?"

"Yes."

"Well, feed him when he comes to. Underdone beef, if you can. And make him take some whisky — help tide him over any nerve shock. Matter of fact, think I'll prescribe some of that for myself. The Glasgow still doing business?"

"My treat," Mulchay offered. "Mulchay's treat all around." He put an arm around the shoulders of his two cronies, looked back for a moment to the girl. "Be back soon," he told her. "We'll discuss the situation when the lad's himself again." The old men went out, leaving Billy Neale behind.

"What is it between you and him?" the cowboy asked.

"I don't know, Billy," Rosemarie answered.

"Kind of acting like a calf, ain't you?"

"Am I?"

"You sure are! And you sure can't be serious — not serious about taking up with some homeless drifter!"

"He has a home. And a job."

"Yeah, some home! Up in the Negras. You got any idea what it's like up there?"

"Lonely," she said.

"Not for a wildcat, it ain't. Animals like it up there."

"Meaning Tom is no better than an animal?"

"Damn it all — I don't relish talking

about a man when he's out and under like he is. But I got to talk sense into you before it's too late."

"Maybe you're jumping to conclusions, Billy. He told me once tonight he wasn't interested in taking me along."

"You mean you *asked* him? *Him?*"

"Ay. And he turned me down."

"Well, try me then! I wouldn't turn you down."

"That's very sweet of you, Billy."

"Is it the mountains? You figure you'd like to spend some time up there? I'll live with you anywheres, Rosemarie."

The girl laughed at his earnestness.

"So I'm funny. All I am is funny."

"No, no, no! You're a sweet, good-hearted fellow. And tonight I saw just how quick in the mind you are, rushing Mr. Smith back here with the keys. And brave, opening that door in the face of all those guns! You're not funny, Billy Neale. You're a fine man, and some day you'll be the biggest rancher in the Big Bend."

It was quite a speech, and he looked at her for several moments without saying anything.

"I'm all those things, but you want him?"

She returned his steady gaze, nodding her head.

"Suppose he lives in the mountains because he's on the dodge?"

"Oh, no, he couldn't be a criminal. I'd know that about him in the first instant."

"All right, maybe not a criminal, but suppose he's wanted, like those gunmen wanted him tonight. What kind of life would that be for a woman?"

"I've already told you," she said patiently. "He's turned me down."

"But you're not going to take no for an answer. Is that it?"

"What's all the shouting about?" the rumbling voice of Buchanan asked, startling them both badly.

"How long you been awake?" Neale asked him gruffly.

"Awake? How long've I been out?"

"Not long enough," Rosemarie told him worriedly. "How does your poor shoulder feel?"

"Tender. How'd I wind up here — and where's the little guy?"

"You're in Mr. Smith's shop," she told him. "Mr. Mulchay is fine."

"That Captain Gibbons was here a while ago," Billy Neale said then. "He gave you what he called safe conduct out of town."

"Yeah?"

"It's good for twenty-four hours, Gibbons said."

"Hope somebody thanked him for me."

"You gonna take it?"

"The safe conduct?"

"Yeah."

"I don't know about that," Buchanan said thoughtfully. "But one thing sure — I've got to be on my way before any twenty-four hours . . ."

"You couldn't!" Rosemarie objected. "Not possibly, Tom!"

He regarded the girl with a face that was expressionless, then a smile broke through and he glanced at Neale.

"You have trouble gettin' this one to agree with anything you say?"

"With most everything."

"But of course you can't go anywhere," Rosemarie insisted. "Not for weeks! What in the world are you doing?"

What Buchanan was doing was rolling on his good shoulder and pushing himself up. The girl stepped forward and put both hands on his chest.

"Lie back down there this instant!" she commanded.

But it was as though she weren't there as he swung his legs over the edge of the cot.

"Lie down!" she ordered again.

"You're bad wounded!"

He stood up, and even Neale watched that with open wonder. His daddy's legends of the Territory giants of fifty years ago were coming true before his eyes.

"Better take it easy, Buchanan," he told him doubtfully. "Don't push your luck."

"Don't push what luck? I was in pretty fair shape till I came down here."

"Please, Tom, lie *down*," Rosemarie asked him plaintively.

"Man, just look at my duds," Buchanan said, observing for the first time that half his shirt was cut away, that only one trouser leg was intact. "Town looked so peaceful, too, from the mountain."

"I'll outfit you," Neale said, bridling at the disparagement of Scotstown. "But don't blame the folks here for your troubles. It came from outsiders, just —"

"Just what?" Buchanan asked him. "Outsiders just like myself?"

"True, ain't it? You're a stranger, and all of them are strangers. You just happened to pick this town to fight it out."

"Billy!"

"Well, that's what happened, isn't it?" Neale replied to the girl. "This is quiet, decent cattle country. Everybody works hard and takes time out Saturday night.

Fistfights, sure. But a man don't take a gun into town." He paused, stared defiantly at Buchanan. "I'm twenty-eight years old," he said, "and you're the first man I ever knew that killed another — that ever even pointed a loaded gun at another."

"Billy — stop!" Rosemarie cried. "He did what he had to do tonight. They gave him no choice . . ."

"No," Buchanan said, his voice calm against the charged emotion of theirs. "I had a choice. In the saloon I could have walked out, like the proddy told me to. In the dancehall I had even less excuse. I pointed a loaded gun at that son, whoever he was, for no better reason than I was sore at him."

"I talked without thinking, Buchanan," Billy Neale said. "Sorry."

"Not as much as I am. Also much obliged, which is more important. Damned if I could have kept opening that door."

"You would."

"I don't know," Buchanan said. "A man likes to think he would, but I don't know."

"It was a wonderful, brave thing," Rosemarie added.

"And I'm living proof of it," Buchanan said. "I was there!"

"If you're trying to pull my stinger,

mister," Neale said, then smiled, "well, you've done it. I'll go see what I can do about a shirt and pants." He looked the big man over again and shook his head. "Going to fit damn quick, I promise you that."

The cowboy left, and left a silence behind him. Not a tranquil, comfortable sort of quiet, but an electric one, charged with the woman's awareness of the bare-waisted man and his awareness of her interest.

Rosemarie spoke into it, uneasily.

"Even if you get another outfit," she said, "you can't travel anywhere. Not yet, Tom."

"You don't happen to smoke, do you?" Buchanan asked.

"Smoke?"

"Somewhere along the line," he said wistfully, "I lost my makings. A little tobacco would be fine right now."

"Would there be any in a hardware shop?" Rosemarie wondered, momentarily untracked from her main subject — as he had intended.

"Not likely."

"I'll ask for some in the Glasgow," she offered. "You wait right here, now."

"I'll wait."

Neale returned first, bringing a rider's work shirt of durable flannel and twill trousers with reinforced knee pads.

"These are brand new," Buchanan said, feeling the cloth respectfully.

"Bought 'em this evening," Neale admitted. "Must've had a premonition."

"How much they set you back?"

"Bought 'em at the company store. Forget about it."

"Ten dollars?"

"Not half. Where's Rosemarie?"

"Beggin' me some tobacco."

"Hell, I got some. Here."

"Got my own, thanks."

"Then how come —"

"Just hoping you'd get back first," Buchanan explained, peeling off the remnants of the trousers with an effort, having to sit down on the cot again while he slowly put his legs through the new ones.

"You're really going to leave tonight?"

"Got to."

"And you're afraid she'll hold you back?"

Buchanan pushed himself to his feet and pulled the shirt around his shoulders. As Neale had warned, the outfit was snug. He began to button it across his chest, laboriously, when the cowboy realized there had been no answer to his question.

"Must be tough, Buchanan — girl like Rosemarie throwing herself at you."

The tall man continued to dress himself,

stuffed the shirttail deep into the trousers, still not answering. But then his eyes lost their preoccupied look and focused intently on Neale's face.

"You bet it's tough," he said, almost threateningly. And that was all he said, leaving the other man puzzled.

"I'd trade places with you," Neale said.

"And do what different?" Buchanan asked, moving slowly across the small room to the desk where Smith kept his books. He found a marking pencil there and a sheet of yellow paper.

"I'd take her with me," Neale said. "Wherever I was going."

"No you wouldn't," Buchanan told him without interrupting his writing. "Not if you'd ever been where I'm going." He straightened up then, carried the paper back to Neale, and handed it to him. *To Mr. B. Neale,* it read. *I.O.U. ten (10) dollars gold, U.S.A. currency. T. Buchanan.*

"You're a stubborn son," Neale told him.

"Must be." He held out his big hand. "So long, Billy Neale," he said.

Neale shook the hand. "Where's your horse at? I'll walk you there."

"Had a horse four months ago," Buchanan said. "Traded him for a burro team —" he

110

grinned — "and the burros died on the mountain."

Neale shook his head. "Man, you're really hard up, aren't you?"

"Not according to my partner. He tells me I'm worth a couple of million, at least. See you in church," he said from the doorway, and limped out.

Scotstown was quiet now, the street deserted, and the only light still glowing came from the Glasgow. As Buchanan glanced that way the swinging doors parted and Rosemarie came onto the street, her head bent in earnest conversation with Angus Mulchay. He watched her come on for another moment, long enough to make her image indelible, and then slipped out of sight around the corner of the building. He went that way until he reached the next street, swung south and headed for the towering black mass that was the mountain.

You bet it's tough, he said, but nobody heard him.

NINE

Going to church on Sunday morning was an integral part of the life in Scotstown, and it would be safe to estimate that on this particular sunny Sunday in June some ninety per cent of the town's three hundred-odd population were attending services in the handsome new building Malcolm Lord had been so instrumental in erecting.

And because the rancher was such a prominent member of his congregation, the Reverend Jamieson was willing to forego his regular sermon and permit Lord the use of the pulpit for what the minister had been told was an important, though nonsacred, message. That, as a matter of fact, was what Dr. Jamieson told the congregation by way of introduction — and Angus Mulchay, who had been settling down for the half-hour nap he always took at this time Sunday, suddenly sat up straight in his pew, eyes wary and suspicious.

Malcolm Lord made a fine figure in the

pulpit, handsome in a distinguished manner, affluent and benign, aristocratic, even, and there were few there besides Mulchay who didn't feel prouder of themselves because this was their good neighbor, their benefactor and first vestryman.

Lord thanked Dr. Jamieson and took a sweeping glance at the upturned faces of Scotstown.

"My friends," he told them in his sure, rich-toned voice, "I am going to speak to you of two matters. One of them is the unpleasantness that occurred within our peaceful community last evening. For those who may not yet have heard, there was a common gunfight in Mr. Terhune's otherwise perfectly respectable establishment. A man, unfortunately, was shot to death — the first such casualty in our town since the board of councilmen appointed the present sheriff.

"More unfortunately still, there was a second gunfight — brought on by the first as such things generally happen — and other casualties. No Scotstown man, I am deeply gratified to say, was involved in either fight . . ."

"The hell he says!" Mulchay whispered indignantly and irreverently, earning for himself a dozen hostile glares.

". . . although one of Overlord's young men, Billy Neale, was instrumental in ending the disturbance. Now you may wonder why I asked Dr. Jamieson to speak of last night's trouble to you all on this, the day of prayer. The reason, my friends, is that some of the men who did take part in the shootings were in Scotstown at my own personal instigation. Therefore, I take full responsibility for everything that happened, and will make complete restitution for all property damage that occurred.

"Now who were these men? They are Texas soldiers — cavalry troopers, to be exact — and they are members of that elite and courageous corps known as Gibbons' Militia. This group, formed a year ago by the famous Ranger Captain, John Gibbons, are becoming famed far and wide for the great and valorous service they perform along our strife-torn border.

"These few, the cream of Texas manhood, have stepped into the breech where our do-nothing state and federal governments have left us to defend ourselves against another Mexican invasion . . ."

"Invasion!" echoed a startled lady in the rear.

"Ay, invasion, Mrs. Watkins. Did you think they had given up just because a treaty was signed? Did you believe they wouldn't really make a try to conquer Texas again, put us under the rule of a foreigner? My friends, in this house of holy worship I will not say more of what an invasion will mean — I will not conjure up pictures in your minds of what the invaders will do to our fair sex when all the men have been tortured and killed.

"But we are in imminent peril of being attacked. Their advance patrols already come and go across the border with impunity. These scouts spy us out, choose their future victims for the main attack . . ."

"Merciful heavens!" Mrs. Watkins said, and there were other ladies now to join her in voicing fear.

"But be assured," Lord went on, his voice rising. "You will be saved! Captain Gibbons and his militia are taking up defensive positions along the river this very minute —"

"What's that?" Mulchay demanded, not whispering.

"Even as I speak to you," Lord went on, "the protectors of Scotstown are routing out the advance patrols, driving the transgressors back to their own land . . ."

"Wait a minute, Malcolm Lord!" Mulchay shouted, on his feet now. "Do you mean to stand there and say you've sent

Black Jack Gibbons down to my property? To MacKay's?"

"The militia is here for the safety and protection of us all, Angus Mulchay! If you are providing Mexican raiders a route by which Scotstown will be sacked — then I accuse you of endangering the lives of every man, woman and child among us!"

"So say we all!" somebody cried in emotional support.

"Ay!" chimed in others. "Ay!"

"Mulchay would have us all slaughtered!"

But Mulchay was already hurrying out of the church, leaving Malcolm Lord a clear victory in his campaign for public opinion.

The invading hordes totaled eight happy-go-lucky *bandidos* whose total armament was three rifles, four handguns, and eating knives all around. Their leader was a fierce-looking fat man named Ramon, whom none of them obeyed but who was *jefe* nevertheless because he owned the best rifle — a Remington that Mulchay had sold him two years before.

They were thieves by occupation, just as their fathers and grandfathers had been — too proud to beg, too childlike to work — and most skilled in the allied arts of lying, lovemaking and consuming *vino*. Angus

Mulchay thought the thing they did best of all was sleep; sleep a minimum of ten hours in any twenty-four, sleep the clock around, sleep in the middle of a conversation.

And they were sleeping this Sunday morning, all over the lush grass that constituted the yard behind Mulchay's six-room ranch house, but they had earned their rest, having spent almost the entire night in the saddle eluding the *federales* chasing them from San Carlos. It had been a hard ride for poor profit, the state of Chihuahua becoming more and more policed, less and less a freebooter's paradise, but they had reached their *yanqui* sanctuary safely and even if they had no gold this time, Señor Angus would be good for a handout.

The advance patrol of Gibbons' Militia damned near ran over them.

"For crissake, are they dead?" "Trooper" Glines asked "Sergeant" Lou Kersh, reining his mount sharply.

"Let's see," Kersh said, sliding the .45 into his fist, pumping three booming shots into the ground beside the sombrero-shaded head of Ramon. The fat man came awake as quickly as it was possible for him — some several seconds later than Mario and José, who slept nearby. Within another half-minute all eight were rubbing their eyes sleepily, struggling to sitting positions.

"Qué pasa? Qué pasa?" began the bewildered chorus. "What the hell goes on?"

Kersh answered gutturally, "Get up, you sorry bastards! On your miserable feet!"

The command, accompanied by the hard faces of the mounted men all around them, the drawn guns, made no sense at all but had a great deal of meaning. They got up, hands above heads.

"You make a mistake, amigo," Ramon said, addressing himself to his opposite number. "We are *invitados* — guests of the Señor Angus."

"Line up!" Kersh ordered, swinging his .45 with a negligent menace. "Get in next to the fat one. *Al lado del gordo!*" he repeated in his border-Mexican, and they formed a ragged line beside Ramon.

At the sound of the staccato gunfire Black Jack Gibbons had sunk spurs into his horse almost involuntarily, and swung the animal's head in the direction of Mulchay's place with an expectant kind of excitement running through him.

He raced toward the house, some three hundred yards away, and watched with satisfaction as Kersh herded the quarry together. He was happy that Kersh had flushed the first of them. A tonic for the man's morale after last night's sorry business.

"Well, Sergeant, what've we got here?" he asked, pulling his horse close in beside Kersh's, raking the hapless Ramon and his band with a contemptuous glance.

"Murderers and rapists, from the looks of 'em," Kersh said, staring directly at Ramon.

"But no, amigo! No," Ramon said. "Such things we have never done. The Señor Angus, he will tell you we are guests. We come for peace and quiet . . ."

"We got witnesses," Kersh said. "We know all about you. Fat man, you're gonna hang for your sins."

"Hang? *Por Dios,* why? What have I done here?"

"That one, too," Gibbons said, having picked out another brown-skinned face that displeased him, pointing to nineteen-year-old Mario.

"No, amigos, no!" Ramon cried out again. "Surely you are joking?"

"How about him?" Kersh asked, pointing his own arm at a stiletto-slim figure who was a man named Gio Alavarez.

"And him," Gibbons said, singling out a fourth candidate. "We'll take the other four into town."

At a wave of Kersh's head the six

mounted men of his squad moved their horses forward, crowded in on the four who had been condemned, suddenly dropped nooses over their heads, and tightened them brutally.

"No, no!" Ramon shrieked at them. "This cannot be —" A jerk of the rope around his neck cut short the protest.

"Where?" Kersh asked Gibbons. "The cottonwoods by the river?"

"They'd do," Gibbons said. "But this is the loudmouth's range — Mr. Mulchay's. Let's make it a little more personal, Kersh. String 'em up under those eaves."

And that was what the old man found when he reached home — four friends hanging dead by their necks on the front porch of his house. One by one he cut them down, and spent the whole long afternoon digging graves in the earth and burying them decently. Then, far into the night, he carved a common headboard into a thick strip of oak. *Under here,* it read, *Lie Ramon, Mario, Gio and Carlos. Murdered this Sunday, the 13th of June, 1857, by The Butcher of Brownsville.*

TEN

"Well, say!" Fargo said, waking that morning to find Buchanan in camp. "When did you get back up here?"

"Along about dawn."

"Have yourself a real time?"

"So-so."

"Live little town, is it?"

"Live enough. Fargo, I don't have your tobacco."

"You don't?"

"Nor your bottle."

"Well, hell — so long as you had some fun with the money . . ."

"Had to bury a man with it," Buchanan told him.

"No foolin'? How'd he come to die?"

"One of those things. How about some breakfast?"

"Sure thing."

Breakfast was bacon and potatoes, washed down with powerful Mexican coffee brewed from beans they roasted themselves.

The partners ate in silence, and when they were done Buchanan took the tin plates and cups to clean them in the spring just below the camp.

"Notice you move awful stiff," Fargo told him when he returned. "And you're limpin'."

"Got myself shot up some."

"By the gent you buried?"

"No. That one died of over-confidence. Had me pegged for a sheepherder, or something."

"But he had friends along?"

"I don't know whether he had friends or what. They all belonged to some kind of organization." He had the day's first cigarette made and Fargo struck a match for him.

"So you didn't have a good time at all," the old man said, sounding as unhappy about it as if it had been himself.

Buchanan caught the note of sadness and grinned.

"Had my moments, too," he told Fargo. "Drank something called Scot's whisky — not much kick to it."

"I tasted some once, over in Frisco."

"And danced with a good-lookin' woman," Buchanan said, watching Fargo's face brighten.

"Well, that's more like it! She have a bosom?"

"She had everything she ought to — and the whitest teeth you ever saw."

"Good for her. Got to walk her home, didn't you?"

"No."

"How come?" Fargo asked, crestfallen again, and Buchanan wished now he'd embroidered, given the old-timer something to think about during the lonely nights.

"I would have," he amended. "Had it all fixed in my mind to walk her home."

"But why didn't you?"

"Because that's when I got plugged," he answered apologetically.

"Damn their hides, anyhow! Say — you wasn't even armed!"

"Borrowed as I went along."

"What kind of town they runnin' down there, I'd like to know," said the outraged Fargo. "Fella comes down to put a little money into circulation and they shoot him! You weren't drunk and disorderly, were you?"

"Hell, I didn't have time. All I played was just one hand of draw — and you should've seen that, Fargo. Go in with a pair of ladies and wind up with queens full."

"Man, I'll bet that took the pot."

"No."

"No! Somebody beat a full house — full of queens?"

"That's what the man claimed."

"Oh," Fargo said. "The one you buried. Now I'm beginnin' to get the straight of it. Town's full of tinhorns . . ."

Buchanan shook his head again. "The town's fine," he said. "Couldn't be friendlier. But you ever hear of a Captain Gibbons? Black Jack Gibbons?"

"That's somehow familiar," Fargo said, pulling at his ear reflectively. "Sure it is. Seems to me there was saloon talk around Paso last winter, just before I hooked up with you. Fella named Gibbons was recruitin' a private army. Gonna start a new war with Mexico, or somethin' crazy like that."

"What's he got against Mexicans?"

"Don't like chili and beans, maybe. Hell, who knows why some people always got it in for others?"

"I guess," Buchanan said, snubbing the butt beneath his heel. "Well, I came back to mine gold. Better get at it."

"Not in your shape," Fargo said. "Shouldn't even've come back so soon."

"Stiff, is all," the big man said, but Fargo noted that he hefted the pickax left-handed.

"Should be down there in a feather bed," he said.

"You don't know the worst of it," Buchanan said mock-seriously. "Black Jack Gibbons run me out of town."

"The hell he did."

"I'm here."

"I know why you're here, Buchanan. Listen, I've had you under close watch for five hard months. Got you figured complete."

Buchanan laughed at him. "That's just twice the figuring I've done in thirty years . . ."

". . . and if it weren't on account of me you'd never have climbed back up this God-forsaken mountain."

Buchanan laughed again. "If it weren't on account of you, you fast-talking old spell-binder, I'd still be in El Paso."

"Doin' what?"

"As little as the law allows."

"Maybe you're right at that. Maybe you don't know half what you should about yourself."

"No argument there. Come on, let's get to work."

"Forget work," Fargo said. "If last night was Saturday then this is Sunday. And on Sunday the Lord rested. Now, if you were in

El Paso do you know what you'd be doin'?"

"Resting, just like every other day."

"Like hell!"

"Then what?"

"Makin' other men richer than they were, that's what! Boy, you just don't have the first idea about yourself. A man with some plan in his mind, some project to pull off — he sees you and you're hired. It's good as done."

"Some project like axing a mountain down to sea level?"

"Sure! Or somethin' simple, like ramroddin' somebody's herd to Cimmaron without losin' a head. Or ridin' shotgun out of Nevada City . . ."

"Those jobs still open?"

"They sure as hell are, and will be. And you'd've been sucked right into 'em, layin' down your life to make another man rich."

"Well, you saved me from that, old friend."

"You're damn right I did! You're working for you, now, Buchanan. Every time you swing that pick you're making your own self richer."

"Then let's get swinging," Buchanan suggested.

"On the Lord's Day? God damn it, boy, don't you read your scripture?"

"I'll catch up on it when I've made myself rich, like you just said I would."

"All right, all right," Fargo said, going for the small, sharp-nosed hammer he used to separate the gold-bearing veins from the blocks that Buchanan axed out of the mountainside. "But this is the day He rested, and so should we!"

They worked all day, and that night Buchanan crawled gratefully into his blankets hurting and exhausted — too weary even to consider a return visit to Scotstown. Which was exactly as he had planned it.

ELEVEN

∩

The first fifteen days of its occupation of the Big Bend's river ranches, Gibbons' Militia had summarily hung nine "invaders," killed twelve "escapees" out of hand, and imprisoned twenty more in the hastily erected, barbed-wire compound on the outskirts of town. Helpfully to the campaign that Malcolm Lord kept telling his fellow citizens about, some half-dozen of the prisoners had actually been apprehended in the act of rustling four head of Angus Mulchay's small herd. Unlike the others who had been taken before them, these Mexicans could not plead that Mulchay had invited them to take the beef. In the eyes of all Scotstown they were plainly guilty of a hanging offense — inasmuch as Mulchay had left the Big Bend two weeks before.

At Lord's suggestion, Gibbons allowed the hapless rustlers to be tried in open court. It had all the trappings and appearances of a fair, Texas-style trial, except that

Lou Kersh made a surprising appearance for the defense — as court interpreter — and he managed to "interpret" some very damaging admissions for the accused men without the jury fully realizing just who Lou Kersh was.

One of the Mexicans, to cite an example, was telling the jury, via Kersh, that if he were given a chance to go back across the border he would return dutifully to his wife and family. *"Mi mujer y ninos,"* he said.

With a straight face Kersh defined *mujer* rightfully as "woman." And then proceeded to tell the jurors that the man had crossed the border for a woman. Another prisoner explained that he had money to pay Mulchay for the steer, but that Mulchay wasn't at home and hunger got the best of him. *"Yo tuve hambre,"* he told the interpreter plaintively. "I was hungry."

"He says he was hungry for a woman," Kersh said in a loud, clear voice.

The jury deliberated for thirty minutes, and voted them all guilty with no recommendation for mercy. Special Judge Gibbons ordered them to be hanged at sunset — and so it appeared on the trial record duly signed by Councilmen Lord, Butler and MacPike.

That trial — its cloak of rightness and

righteousness — plus the continuing absence of Mulchay — which became a kind of admission of guilt in a conspiracy against his neighbors — persuaded Malcolm Lord to advance the timetable for his master plan to annex the riverland to his Overlord holdings. Two days later squads of Gibbons' Militia began making official calls on the far-flung ranches of Mulchay's friends — the Tompkins, the Alreds, the Bryans and the MacKays.

Captain Gibbons himself led six hostile-looking horsemen to the MacKay place, ordered them to stay mounted while he climbed the porch.

This was a hot, breezeless Tuesday and Rosemarie answered his knock.

"What will you have with us?" she asked through the screened door, holding a hastily-donned wrapper closed at her throat.

"May I come in?" When the man thought it was worth the effort — as he did now — Gibbons could project a very powerful, very virile personality.

"My uncle is not in the house," the girl said. "Perhaps if you returned later . . ."

"My business concerns both of you," Gibbons said, blandly opening the door.

"But what's needed even more urgently is some water. May my men use the well?"

Rosemarie had stepped back into the room, against her will. "Yes, they may," she said in answer to the question.

"Draw yourselves some water," Gibbons called over his shoulder, then crossed the threshold in the casual manner of a familiar visitor. "Ah, it's cool in here," he said. "Very comfortable." He looked at her, wondered what, if anything, she wore beneath the thin cotton robe.

"I have a great many things to do, Captain Gibbons. If you'll come back in the afternoon I'm sure my uncle will be here."

"Does it unsettle you so much — a strange man in your house?"

"I'll not pretend you're welcome here, if that's what you mean."

Gibbons laughed. "Well, that's playing the cards face up," he said lightly, then proceeded to lower himself onto the sofa. "And why am I unwelcome to you?" he asked.

"Because you are an evil man," Rosemarie told him bluntly. "And I want you to leave at once."

Instead of leaving, Gibbons crossed his legs, took a long cigar from a pocket inside his riding coat.

"Either you leave or I do!" the girl said

with heat in her voice. Gibbons lit the cigar carefully, let his glance roam over her face and figure at will.

"I wouldn't walk out into that yard, miss," he said. "If my men thought you were no longer under my special protection . . ."

"I was never under your protection, special or otherwise!"

"Ah, but you are. And so far it's kept you from becoming — how should I say — common property."

Her hand went to her face, as if he had struck her.

"What a horrible, horrible thing for a man to say . . ."

"It wasn't my intention to shock you, girl, but to acquaint you with a fact. Regardless of all the good they're accomplishing here, my men are still soldiers. Any woman would attract them, but with your — ah — endowments . . ."

"Stop it!" Rosemarie cried at him. "Get out of this house without speaking another indecent word!"

"You're very excitable, aren't you?" Gibbons asked, his studied mildness like a goad. "Even more than I'd imagined you'd be."

"I don't want you to imagine anything

about me! I don't want you to think of me in any way, ever!"

"It would be easier to quit breathing altogether."

"Get out!" she ordered him again. "Get away from me!"

No man of Gibbons' ego could take such open reproach indefinitely. Now he climbed to his feet, and the look of mock-amiability dropped from his face, revealing the naked desire that had been there from the moment he had stood in the doorway.

"Another woman in your place," he told her severely, "would be grateful."

"Grateful? If I had a whip in my hands I'd show you my gratitude!"

The words, the scorn, the total rejection — all of it came together against the man's own conceit, and snapped what little was left of his reserve. With a kind of grunting noise deep in his throat he moved toward the girl, reaching out swiftly with both hands. But his eyes had signaled the attack and she stepped backward, swung away from him and broke for the nearby kitchen. Gibbons' grasping fingers caught in a fold of the loose wrapper, closed tight over the light material and wrenched it furiously. The gown, handsewn, was ripped apart, baring the twisting, struggling girl from hip to shoulder. The man held fast, tried to tear it away entirely, and then the girl turned back against him, swung with her considerable strength and caught him flush on the cheekbone with the heel of her open palm.

Gibbons fell back, dazed for that moment, and Rosemarie lashed out at him again. Better to have run, for half the victory in the first blow was its very surprise. Gibbons all but invited the next one, the better to imprison both her arms, to close her half-naked, unyielding body against him.

"Fight me," he said raggedly, his lips pressed to her ear. "The harder you make it, the sweeter the victory . . ."

The girl intended to make it as sweet as she possibly could. Both hands clawed at her tormentor's face, left their mark in his flesh. At the same time she kicked at him, then brought the hands up again, into his hair, tried to pull it loose by the very roots.

Gibbons, in his passion, was immune to pain or indignity. He stripped the robe completely away and bore her back to the divan with a relentlessness that was overpowering.

It was not a silent struggle, and the sounds of it drew the militiamen from their labors at the well to the porch of the house. Not one of them felt any compulsion to interfere. They had all seen the beautiful girl who worked at the Glasgow, and made the same snap judgment as Hamp Leach. That made what was happening to her now a kind of sport — a soldier's pastime — and they envied the man involved.

But one of them, a man named Apgar, chanced to look around, and spotted the two riders bearing down on the place. Two coming on with an unmistakable urgency, and neither one belonging to Gibbons' Militia.

"Look sharp!" Apgar shouted the alarm. "May be trouble!"

"Who the hell are they?"

"May be trouble," Apgar warned again. "Hey Cap — Cap'n Gibbons! Two riders out here!"

Gibbons heard, whirled furiously from the writhing, twisting Rosemarie, and crossed to the door. The animal look was still strong in his face, but as he watched the determined approach of the two horsemen he brought his thoughts to heel.

"Spread yourselves," he ordered. "Get off the porch and fan out around the yard." The bright sun made the pupils of his eyes contract swiftly, and now he could make out one of the riders. The missing old man, Mulchay — and in the moment of recognition he thought he knew where the troublemaker had been and what he was up to.

"Stand fast," Gibbons called to his deploying men. "And by God be ready to fight!" He turned back into the room for a moment then, just as the bitterly sobbing girl ran into her own bedroom. The door slammed shut.

"A good idea, if you stay there," Gibbons said warningly. "If you don't, there may be a life on your hands." He went out of the house to stand at the top of the short flight of stairs, his face and the set of his body defiant.

Angus Mulchay wheeled to a stop below him.

"What are ye doin' here?" the old man asked suspiciously. "Where's the lass?"

"Not at home to callers," Gibbons said, but all his attention was on the other horseman, a grim-visaged character with the look of winter in his eyes and the small silver badge of the Rangers pinned to his shirt front. The man himself was noting the number and disposition of the force spread out in a semicircle around the yard.

"I'll have a word with the lass," Mulchay announced.

"You'll wheel right around, if you know what's best for you," Gibbons said.

"Your day is done on the Big Bend,"

Mulchay answered, continuing to dismount. "Ranger Keroon has your warrant in his pocket."

Seth Keroon and Jack Gibbons had known each other nearly twenty years, but the men they were seeing now were like two strangers. Mulchay hitched his horse to the porch rail and started up the steps. Gibbons raised his booted foot, shoved it against Mulchay's chest, and sent him sprawling in the dust.

"I'm all the law that's needed in the Big Bend," Gibbons said, speaking directly to Keroon. The Ranger squared his shoulders, as if he could feel the weight of the eyes staring intently at his back, the position of his gun hand.

"The governor sent me to bring you up to Austin," he said calmly.

"Sam Bradford's a traitor to Texas," Gibbons answered. "He's betrayed the men who died to free us from Mexico."

"Don't waste that kind of talk on me, Jack," Keroon told him. "You and I understand what you're trying to do down here."

"If you understand that, Seth, you won't try to serve any piece of paper on me."

"But you know I'm going to . . ."

"Come back here, you old fool!" Gibbons

shouted to Mulchay, diverted by the man's attempt to circle to the rear door of the house.

"I mean to see the lass," Angus shouted back. "Somethin' tells me she's had trouble with ye!"

"Apgar!" Gibbons called, and the man nearest to Mulchay drew his gun and stood across the old man's path.

"Let him pass," Seth Keroon ordered in his quiet voice, and Apgar's glance went nervously to the famous badge, then to Gibbons' face for reassurance. He stayed in Mulchay's way.

"I'm all the law that's needed," Gibbons repeated to the Ranger. "Ride out."

"No," Keroon said, then swung so that he faced the tense, expectant men behind him. "I'm here to arrest Jack Gibbons," he told them. "Him alone. If your orders are to interfere, then I rescind them — and I speak for the State of Texas!"

The six of them shifted uneasily. Then one of them spoke.

"Ride out like you were told to, mister. Rangers ain't no special breed to Gibbons' Militia."

Keroon sighed, turned back to Gibbons.

"I arrest you in the name of the people of Texas," he said and reached for the warrant. Some gunman thought he was going for a breast gun. He drew and fired, the slug catching the lawman in the small of the back. Four more times he was hit in that many seconds, the bullets driving him lifeless from the saddle.

"You foul cowards!" Mulchay cried at them. "You miserable butchers —" Apgar raised his gun high, brought it down with sickening force on the man's head. Mulchay went to his knees, fell head down and lay there.

The door at Gibbons' back swung open and Rosemarie stepped onto the porch, dressed again and wide-eyed with terror. Her glance took in the murdered man and the crumpled figure of Mulchay, but when she would have gone to him, Gibbons' arm circled her waist and held her back.

"What have you done?" she demanded brokenly. "What have you done?"

"Get your things together, missy. We're traveling fast . . ."

"No! I won't go with you!"

"You will — or you can stand here and watch Mulchay take a bullet in the back of his head!"

"You wouldn't!"

"Apgar, at the count of three finish the old meddler. One! Two —" The stolid

Apgar thumbed the hammer back.

"No, no!"

"Get packed in three minutes," Gibbons ordered, and the girl re-entered the house. Gibbons then had the dead man and the unconscious one tied across their saddles. Rosemarie came down the steps, carrying a small duffle bag, and a horse from the small remuda was made ready for her. Leaving one man behind to take Lauren MacKay into custody, the strange party rode off.

TWELVE

It was Angus Mulchay's nature to speak and to act impetuously — and on the morning that he had taken it into his mind to ride off to Austin for help, the man had done so without informing any of his friends what he was up to. Naturally, those cronies wondered about him — it was all they talked about during the first few days of his disappearance — but when two weeks had passed without a word, Hamlin, MacIntosh *et al* were of the opinion that a delegation of Gibbons' hardcase army had put the fear of God into him and packed him off.

"He'll be back in the country soon," they told each other confidently.

"Ay, and denyin' that Gibbons was the cause."

And when they gathered at the Glasgow this hot Tuesday evening they had no idea that Mulchay had, indeed, come back. But there were other things to talk about to-night, for the families of the Tompkins, the

Alreds and the Bryans were in town lock, stock and barrel, and the three heads of those families were hopping mad about it.

" 'Load up your wagon, you're moving,' this dirty-faced gunman tells me," Jock Bryan reported to the assemblage in the saloon. " 'And why am I moving?' I asks him. 'Because you're in a battle zone,' he tells me in that surly voice. Imagine! The land I've ranched for twenty-five years is a battle zone!"

"The same as they did to me," Cy Tompkins added. "Only I was told it was for the safety of my family. So I said *I'd* decide about the safety of my family, as I've always done — and he says, no, Captain Gibbons does all the deciding in the Big Bend for everyone."

"Well?" the big-chested Alex Alred demanded. "What are we going to do about Captain High-and-Mighty Gibbons?"

"Turn him and his rascals out!" shouted the usually retiring Bryan. "I'm a Godfearing man, and violence offends me — but there comes a first time for everyone!"

"Ay."

"Gibbons has gone too far! I say we elect a captain of our own. My vote goes to Cy Tompkins."

Alex Alred was the last speaker, and it was not until he had made his nomination that he was aware he was talking into a dead silence. All the excited clamor in the big room had vanished into thin air, and the puzzled man turned slowly around to stare at a trio of militiamen inside the doorway.

"Who is Cy Tompkins?" Lou Kersh asked Alred. "Trot him out here."

"This is a private meeting," Ken Hamlin said.

"It's going to be, as soon as every Mex-lover in the place pulls stakes."

"We're getting a little tired of that," Hamlin countered. "All opposed to Gibbons get tarred with the same old brush."

"As soon as every Mex-lover pulls stakes," Kersh said again, as if the other man hadn't spoken. "Clears out of the country. Now, which one is Cy Tompkins?"

There was a pause, then the man cleared his throat nervously and stepped forward. "My name is Tompkins," he said.

"Do you accept the nomination?"

"What?"

"For captain of the home guard, mister. Are you number one here?"

"Give the fellow some peace," Hamlin protested. "You've already done enough for one day."

"You're the big talker," Kersh told him. "Maybe you're the one they want to rep them."

"Hamlin is not concerned in this. It's my ranch you moved on to." Tompkins walked three strides closer to the three gunmen. "If my friends want me," he said, "I'm their captain."

"All his friends raise their hands," Kersh said, and they all did. Kersh laughed. "Some friends," he said to the other pair and they laughed, too. "All right, Tompkins, let's go."

"Go where?"

"To the calabozo! Where the hell did you think? As of sundown this town's under martial law, and you're looking at the provost marshal."

"But what's Tompkins done?" demanded MacIntosh, outraged.

"What hasn't he done? Aiding and abetting an enemy of the State of Texas, inciting to riot, illegal assembly — Tompkins, you're a dangerous character to be running around loose. Let's go!"

The other two shifted position, gave each other arm room, and there was something not quite sane in the face of Lou Kersh, at least. He wanted them to force his hand.

"I'll go with you," Cy Tompkins said.

"Then take me as well," Jock Bryan volunteered. Alex Alred came forward at the same time.

Kersh shook his head.

"Just one criminal at a time," he said. "But if you're still here rabble-rousing when we get back, the rest will be accommodated."

The three of them left with Tompkins between them.

THIRTEEN

Jack Gibbons' strong point was his talent for improvising. Where another man might have been badly rattled by the unexpected and thoroughly unwanted turn of events at the MacKay ranch, Gibbons had a resilience of mind, a military man's inborn ability to go ice-calm in moments of stress, to think on the spot and by the very confidence he felt in himself quell the fears of others.

For there had been fear there in MacKay's yard, a real anxiety in the hearts of all those who had helped kill a Ranger. Gibbons had sensed it, and reacted with precision and poise. His somewhat remarkable decision was to pretend that the whole thing had never happened, that he and the men had never ridden this way; he had not so much as laid eyes on the girl; Mulchay had never arrived and there was no such person as Seth Keroon.

So he cleared them all out and headed the party west to Mulchay's range, for the same thought process that produced this solution also included the basic proposition that here was the land Malcolm Lord had hired him to usurp.

And always — in all ways — he had the threat of the Mexican invaders.

At Mulchay's house his riders continued to obey his crisply spoken orders, though they had no idea what the purpose was. First they strung up the bullet-riddled body to the same eaves where the four Mexicans had been lynched fifteen days ago. Then the paint Gibbons wanted was found, and he himself got down on hands and knees and swashed the single word on the porch floor beneath the hanging man.

Venganza! it read, each letter crudely stroked, foreign-looking. *Revenge!* Even the dull-witted Harley could spell that out, get the inference that he hadn't pumped a bullet into the Ranger at all. It was those damn Mexicans. But some others, like Apgar, wondered about the eyewitnesses to the actual affair. What was their fast-thinking boss going to do about the unconscious, but still alive Mulchay? And the girl?

Jack Gibbons knew that a little explanation, like knowledge, was a dangerous thing. So he told them what to do.

At sundown Apgar was to set out for the

Overlord spread. He should push his horse every minute of the way. He would find Gibbons at the ranch with Malcolm Lord, and excitedly report an invasion of Mulchay's place from across the river. So much for Apgar.

Riker was to stage the "raid" here. He was to watch the passage of time carefully — and one hour after Apgar started off he was to set fire to the outbuildings, and when they were ablaze put the torch to the main house.

"Cato," Gibbons said then, keeping his voice unemotional, tactical — "Cato, your work is the blabbermouth. You still pack those Mex blades in your saddlebag?"

Cato, a lean and hungry-looking man, nodded.

"Then use one you can part with. Wait until the house is on fire, then drag him out beyond the porch. Leave the knife sticking in his heart where we can all see it."

Cato nodded again.

"After that all four of you clear out. We'll rendezvous at the MacKay ranch. Any questions?"

"That's the Ranger, the house, and the old man," Apgar said. "There's one other."

"She's my problem," Gibbons told him. "You and everybody else forget about her."

He said that with the same assurance he'd

said everything else, turned away from them before they could read the troubled indecision in his eyes. For Rosemarie certainly was his problem, and a mind-torturing one to solve under this kind of pressure. His coldly practical half demanded she be left here with Cato, warned him over and over that she was his damnation. But pride and passion bent him the other way, fed his hungry ego. *The woman is yours,* their strong voice insisted. *A prize of war.* Then, when he wavered again: *What are you afraid of? You do run things. Or do you?*

His thoughts had carried him to the back of the house, where Harley was standing guard over Rosemarie, and the girl in her turn was making Mulchay as comfortable as she could.

As soon as she saw him she stood up, almost by reflex action, and it was the defiance in her, the pure loathing for him that pushed Gibbons into his decision.

"You and I are leaving," he said to her.

"I'm staying with Angus . . ."

His fingers clamped on her upper arm, painfully, and he swung her around and half-dragged her out the rear door.

"You're going to learn one thing," Gibbons promised. "You're going to learn to jump when I tell you to."

He forced her to ride ahead of him along the river, to a line camp Mulchay and his neighbor Bryan shared for their common roundup. Rosemarie was ushered into the small, clapboard shack.

"See you tonight," Gibbons said. "By the light of the silvery moon." He closed the door and bolted it, and rode for Scotstown, there to instruct Lou Kersh about invoking the martial law, then on to Overlord to set the scene for the "invasion" of Mulchay's ranch.

FOURTEEN

Lauren MacKay was a round, bustling, blue-eyed man who always had a great many important affairs to attend to — tomorrow — and what kept him busy today was avoiding doing those things he had spoken of to Rosemarie yesterday. Each morning he arose with the sun, ordered his favorite breakfast of flapjacks and boiled beef, and after the third cup of coffee studiously wrote out a list of chores that was invariably the same as the list he threw away the night before. Then he left the house, looking purposeful, and perhaps his eye would notice that a board was coming loose in the steps. The loose board immediately went on the list — first thing tomorrow — and he would continue his inspection of the ranch.

And that was the man's real occupation, riding endlessly over the six hundred acres he owned. It stunned his imagination, all this grass, filled him with so much awe of the size of it that he couldn't begin to think where he should start working it. But he was going to start — tomorrow — start perhaps with a loan. That way he could increase his herd to, say, five hundred head. And with that much beef he'd have to hire half a dozen punchers, a wrangler and a full-time Mex cook to help his niece with her work. In a year, maybe less, he'd be drawing level with Malcolm Lord — and wouldn't that be something, pestering Lord to buy him out instead of vice versa? Rosemarie, of course, would have to stop working in the saloon and learn to live like a girl with the richest uncle in the Big Bend.

He'd get on it tomorrow, first thing, but by now it was nearly noon, time to head for his favorite spot by the river, where he had the jug cooling and the cottonwoods made a siesta the next best thing to heaven. That's where he was when Jack Gibbons was violating the privacy of his home, and the gunfire that followed startled him awake.

MacKay's first thought, to give the man his due, was for his niece's safety. But his second was for his own, perhaps only natural for a bachelor of fifty-five, and damn providential, and instead of dashing pell-mell toward the house he went that way circuitously, keeping to the dense grove of cypress. All he saw, when he finally had the house in view, was Gibbons' departing group, Rosemarie amongst them and two figures draped over their saddles. It never occurred to him to go to the house now, thereby negating Gibbons' plan to take him in tow. Instead he took up pursuit of the men with his niece.

This, too, he did with caution, just keeping their dust in view along the primitive road toward Mulchay's spread. And when they arrived at Mulchay's, MacKay took cover in the trees again, biding his time to do he knew not what.

Then, obligingly, Rosemarie and Gibbons emerged from the house, and even at this distance MacKay was dismayed to recognize the rough treatment the girl was receiving. MacKay followed along again, watched her imprisonment — and with maddening precaution waited the better part of twenty minutes before venturing forth to unbolt the door.

And as he slid the bar back — in all fairness to MacKay: the harmless old do-nothing considered it a simple enough business he was engaged in, rather foolish, in fact — but should he live among the angels through eternity the man would never again be on the receiving end of such a look as Rosemarie gave him when he opened that cabin to daylight.

For she had spent every second of those twenty minutes futilely searching a way out of the gloomy little place. Twenty minutes is a large slice of life under those conditions, when even something as drastic as suicide is denied a person, and had the door opened four hours after Gibbons had thrown her in there she could not have felt so heart-burstingly happy to see whose face it was peering in and asking, "What you doin' in there, lass? Come on out."

She couldn't answer, only fly to him, hold onto him as if she needed the feel of his bewhiskered face against hers, the touch of his rough shirt beneath her fingers to make sure this was no dream.

MacKay had no idea what it was all about.

"You better quit that job in Terhune's," he said parentally. "I don't approve the company you meet there."

"I will, Uncle Lauren, I will. But Mr. Mulchay's in trouble. He's bad hurt. We have to help him."

"I've known Angus Mulchay for twenty years. He's forever in trouble."

"But this time it's awful. They mean to kill him off."

"Who does?"

154

"Those gunmen Gibbons left behind."

"Gibbons? The fella that's massacreein' the poor Mexicans?"

"The same. Come on, Uncle, we've got to help."

MacKay spread his arms. "How?" he asked.

How? Rosemarie heard the question echo in her mind and she came back to hard reality, saw her mild-faced uncle for the lovable but still woefully ineffective man he was.

"What can we do?" MacKay asked, reading her dismay.

"Ride with me back to our place," the girl said.

"Why?"

"So you'll be safe, and I can borrow your horse."

"And do what?" he asked, suspicious of her tone. "Nothing foolish, now!"

She shook her head. "Nothing foolish."

"What *are* you going to do?"

"Climb up there," she told him, looking toward the mountain.

"Climb the Negras? And whatever for?"

"For a man," she said. "Now let's be off, both of us."

FIFTEEN

"What day did you say this was?" Fargo asked.

"Tuesday."

"Still June?"

"July the second. The year is eighteen fifty-seven."

"Don't have to bite a man's head off. Hell, I know what year it is."

"I'm not so damn sure."

"Is that so?"

"Yeah, that's so. And I'm not so damn sure about something else."

"And what might that be, Mr. Grouchbag Buchanan?"

"All right, Fargo. I'm a grouchbag and I'm gripin' — but, dammit, tell me one thing: Have you ever in your life mined gold before?"

"You can bet your wasted life I have! Man, I was cashin' nuggets big as California plums ten years before the big strike!"

"Out of a goddam mountain?"

"Well, no. My specialty heretofore was placer minin'. But when I won this here map in a poker game over to El Centro . . ." Fargo's voice trailed away guiltily and he pretended trouble with his full-glowing pipe. The silence dragged on and Buchanan let him fry in his own fat. Finally he turned to look at him.

"You mean the map the old Spanish don gave your granddaddy in seventeen-eighty?" he asked softly. "The one that'd been in the family vault for so long, but because Grandpa saved the don's daughter from drowning herself in the Conchos he handed over the most fabulous treasure in all history? *That* map?"

"That map," Fargo admitted, and when Buchanan broke into wonderful laughter it was one of the most relieving sounds the old man had heard in a lifetime of narrow squeaks.

"Won it in a poker game!" Buchanan was shouting to the moon overhead. "Won — it — in — a — poker — game!"

"Well, it's gold-bearing, ain't it?"

"Sure it is. Sure!" He couldn't or wouldn't bottle the laughter bubbling from his chest. "Gold all the way down, so far as I know. But Fargo, a man can't beat a mountain to death!" A fresh wave of laughter took him and he let himself fall flat on his back. "Won it in a poker game!" he roared happily.

"What's so blinkin' funny about that?"

"The two of us," Buchanan answered him, recovering himself. "You for risking your good money to win it, then turning right around and roping me into the deal."

"Figure you've been chummed, do you?"

"I'm full-grown and long-weaned, old buddy. You took me with my eyes wide open."

"Maybe you'd like to match me for your half of this bonanza — winner take all?"

"Not on your life. The way my luck's running I'd win this damn desolation."

"Desolation, hell! This mountain's worth twenty million to somebody. Fifty."

"Even more, Fargo. But not in our time, not for twenty years. That somebody's going to have to spend half a million to get it out."

"Then let's sell it to him."

Buchanan grinned. "You're the bottle with the cork pulled," he assured him. "Sell what to him? What is it you figure we own?"

"We're here, ain't we? The federal government itself says a man that squats on something long enough has rights, don't it?"

"Rights to live on it, to work it. He can't sell it — and in the second place whole mountains are excluded. That I'm sure —" His voice broke off sharply and he swung to his feet in a lithe, one-piece motion.

"What's the matter?" Fargo asked.

"We got a visitor," Buchanan said, striding to his warbag.

"The cat?"

"Too noisy for her." He slid a rifle free from the bag, cradled it in his arm and crossed the clearing at a right angle to where the sound had come from.

"I don't hear nothin'," Fargo said, but by then Buchanan had slipped from sight over the ridge. Fargo went to his own belongings, produced a formidable Greener, and was soon out of sight in the opposite direction.

Rosemarie was certain that not even in the wildest regions of her rugged Scotland was there such a fearsome place as the Sierra Negras. At the start of her climb it had been the trees, so thick they all but blotted out the midday sun, so close together a person had to detour to find a way between. And down there snakes and a whole world of slithering things made each new step forward an adventure in itself. For an hour you worked along in that company, then the trees grew sparser, the shade diminished and the torrid sun beat down. But the heat was a minor discomfort compared to the bramble bushes — thigh-high they grew, like rolls of barbed wire piled one atop the other, and their bristling defiance of free passage was nature at her thorniest best against the trespass of the animal — in Rosemarie's sorry case, human species.

But a determined person could get past the brambles, paying for it with legs scratched and bloodied from ankle to knee, cotton skirt shredded to ribbons, and could survive that and then find the going really hard. For now the mountain inclined sharply, became a bare wall of rock studded with sharp outcroppings, and climbing it was a test of sheer endurance combined with the surefootedness of a cat.

Of which there were plenty, thriving unmolested as they did in this natural habitat. But night is the time when cats hunt, and though half a dozen terrified the girl with their grunts and snarls, none made the effort to molest the strange-scented game on such a warm, lazy day.

Up she went, slowly, precariously, and after another hour the mountain relented, grew gradually less inclined as if paying a grudging reward. Soon she could see the top, a hundred feet beyond, and she stopped and called his name.

There was no answer. She called it again. Oh, no, she thought dismally. He can't have gone away.

She continued on — thirty more feet, fifty, seventy-five — and that was when Buchanan caught the first sound of her approach and moved defensively to apprehend whoever it was.

And then she called a third time.

"Tom! Tom Buchanan! Oh, where are you?"

"Right behind you," he said and she nearly fell to the ground from the start it gave her. His hand steadied her, and the reassuring strength of that made the girl want to collapse again, but for a different reason. As it was she leaned her head against his chest and relief came in the form of quiet tears.

"Who's with you?" Buchanan asked.

"No one."

"You climbed up here all by yourself? What in the world for?"

"Angus Mulchay. Gibbons has him. They're going to kill him."

"Hey, whatcha got there, boy?" Fargo cried excitedly, breaking from his cover and coming up to them quickly. "By damn!" he said admiringly, drinking in his first sight of womankind in nearly six months.

"This is Fargo, Rosemarie. He's not really as foolish as he looks right now."

Fargo heard the reprimand and quit his wide-eyed inventory.

"This is the good-lookin' gal you danced with down there?"

"This is her. Camp's around this way," he said to Rosemarie. "You can get some rest there and something to eat."

"There's no time," she protested weakly. "We've got to get back to him."

He had started to lead her to the camp-site, but the girl's strength left her all at once and he just did catch her up. Buchanan carried her the rest of the way, settled her on his blankets, and hardly was she there but her eyes closed in deep sleep.

Fargo peered down at her intently.

"You got yourself a beauty, Buchanan."

"She's not mine," Buchanan answered, kneeling at his warbag.

"No?"

"No."

"Tell her that when she wakes up," Fargo said.

"I won't be here." He was standing now, unrolling his holstered Colt from the wide cartridge belt.

"What's that for? Where you goin'?"

"Ran into an old guy when I was down below," Buchanan said, notching the silver buckle, settling the gun comfortably on his hip. "He's in some kind of trouble."

"You comin' back up again?" Fargo asked quietly, and the two of them looked at each other very steadily.

"Not much future in it, is there?" the tall man asked.

"As much as you are going to find anywhere, Buchanan." Fargo's glance fell to the sleeping girl. "More, I'd say."

"Wrong, Fargo." He crossed the space separating them, extended his hand. "It's been my pleasure, Mr. Johns," he said, lightening the mood with his grin. "Drop in when you're passing through Frisco next time."

"Where'll I find you?"

"Where the loudest music is."

"And the fanciest women?"

"Where else?"

"I'll be there, boy. Save a place at the bar for Fargo."

And so they parted, Buchanan walking off the mountain without a look back, Fargo refilling his Meerschaum, settling down against a post of their dugout to keep vigil over the girl.

The old man felt the tears on his cheeks, warm and moist, before he actually knew he'd shed them. He brushed angrily at both eyes and clamped his teeth down tight on the pipestem.

"What in hell ails you, anyhow?" he asked aloud, furious with himself. "Told you he'd see you in Frisco, didn't he?"

The self-scorn was genuine enough, but it didn't work. Fargo was certain that he had seen Buchanan for the last time, and would hear his voice never again. Not in this life.

SIXTEEN

"Well, what kind of a day has it been, Captain?" Malcolm Lord asked expansively, inhaling deeply on a slim, fragrant *panatella*.

"Just routine, I'm afraid," Gibbons answered, matching the same note of worldliness. "Our work goes forward little by little, but it goes forward."

The conspirators sat facing each other in deep-piled leather chairs in the high-ceilinged study of Lord's house, a roast beef dinner consumed, cigars alight, a pony of good brandy at each of their elbows and the world on the end of a string — a string each man thought he held.

"I expect Mulchay was difficult," Lord said.

"Beg pardon?"

"Angus Mulchay. When you moved him off the land."

"Mulchay? Oh, yes, I recall the fellow now. As a matter of fact, we didn't get to his place at all today."

Lord scowled at that.

"Why not?"

"The heat, I expect. We moved out a family named Tompkins, though. And the Byrons . . ."

"Bryans," Lord corrected.

"That's right, Bryan. And the Alreds. Is that the name?"

"Yes. But Mulchay and MacKay are the important ones. The others can come back to the river in time."

"We'll get to Mulchay and MacKay," Gibbons promised.

"When, man? I've got a herd rounded up and waiting for that grass."

"Malcolm," Gibbons said familiarly, "you'll be able to move your stock down to the river by this time tomorrow night."

"Fine, fine," Lord said. "Say, how does this brandy suit you?"

"I'm afraid brandy is something I know little about."

There was a knock on the door.

"Come," Lord said and it was opened by a servant. A Mexican, curiously enough, who very pointedly did not look at Black Jack Gibbons. "What is it, Pedro?"

"*Un hombre por El Capitan, señor. Muy importante, él dice*" — and though it all concerned Gibbons the speaker would not acknowledge him by a glance.

"A man to see you," Lord told him. "Says it's important."

Gibbons knew as much Mexican as either of them, but he waited for Lord to translate.

"I'll go see what it is," he said, rising.

"Perhaps we'll have him in here," Lord said to that, asserting himself just as Gibbons had hoped he would. "More privacy."

"Just as you say, Malcolm."

"Bring the man to me here," Lord ordered and the servant departed, returned quickly with Apgar — who had ridden hard all the way and looked it.

"What is it, Corporal?" Gibbons asked him brusquely.

"We're in for it, Captain," the talented Apgar told him anxiously. "The Mex are coming across in force."

"An attack?"

"Like a horde of locusts, Captain. The men want you."

"By God, let's go!" Gibbons said militantly. "Where have the murdering bastards struck?"

"At Mulchay's, sir! That's where they're hitting us hard."

"Wait, Gibbons!" Lord cried as the other man was hurrying through the doorway. "I'll get some men and come with you!"

"The militia can fight its own battles, Malcolm."

"But if you're outnumbered!"

"We've taken them on at twenty-to-one. We can do it again." He abruptly broke off the conversation, stormed down the hall and out of the house with great determination.

But Malcolm Lord wanted to be in on everything that was happening, wanted a directing hand. He told Pedro to get Foreman Southworth immediately. Pedro shook his head.

"He is not here, señor. The men they are at roundup."

Lord had forgotten.

"They're all out?"

"I think the Mister Billy is here," Pedro said. "The Mister Southworth left him to manage. And there are maybe three others in the bunkhouse."

"Get them, then. And tell Neale to arm everyone and bring a horse around for me. Pronto!"

They came around, four of them, pronto.

"What's up, Mr. Lord?" Billy asked.

"There's trouble down at the river. At Mulchay's. The Mex are trying to take over."

"Take over what, sir?"

168

"The land, the people — Texas! What in hell did you think, Neale?"

Billy held his peace and his tongue. He hadn't been in town since that wild Saturday night, what with all the special movement of the herds, but word had drifted up to Overlord about the war being fought by Gibbons' Militia. He'd grown up with Mexicans, known them all his life around Scotstown, but not until two weeks ago had he heard what dangerous, double-dealing buggers they really were. Funny they should change just like that.

"Ride, Overlord!" Malcolm Lord shouted, leading four apprehensive, uncomfortably armed, and thoroughly unwarlike cowboys out of the plaza and downtrail toward the river.

SEVENTEEN

The sun was just setting over the land when Buchanan found Rosemarie's pegged-out horses at the base of the mountain and rode one of them west along the riverside — the only knowledge he had for the location of Mulchay's place. There was still some aching stiffness in his shoulder, and the saddle chafed the thigh wound, but he was riding again and he felt like a man who has come home after a long trip.

Darkness came on swiftly and presently he came to a fork in the main road. With the aid of a match he read a signpost there: *MacKay Ranch — Lauren MacKay, Owner*, and went on again thoughtfully, not welcoming the reminder of the girl. To his right was the outline of a house, its windows darkened, but in his mind he saw them lightened by lamps, curtained, and a tall, full-bodied girl making a home of it.

Her man would be a rancher, and he'd work hard at it because that was the only thing he wanted — plus her. Each year he'd build the house a little bigger — have to, with kids running around in it — and the herd would get bigger, big enough for two drives a year, and when her man went into Scotstown to cut the dust and play a little table-stakes poker — why, the president of the bank would tip his hat politely and every merchant along Trail Street would come out of his store and wave real friendly.

Great life in store for somebody, Buchanan thought. "Come on, horse, move it!" he said aloud, giving the mare a squeeze of his knees. Who the hell cared about bank presidents?

On and on he rode along the seemingly endless trail, and now he began to worry that he had passed Mulchay's place in the night Hell, it must be two hours since he started.

A bright glow suddenly lit up the night. Fire — the most dreaded sight in a summer so infernally dry as this one. He dug his heels into the mare's sides now and she responded with the fastest spurt she had.

The fire came from an outbuilding beyond the main house, but even as Buchanan was racing toward it he saw a figure running toward that house with a flaming torch in his hand.

Buchanan swept the rifle free and fired it from the crook of his elbow. He hadn't expected a hit and didn't get one — but the arsonist was made aware that he had company coming, and the way he just stood there told Buchanan he hadn't expected any from this direction.

Those seconds of indecision cost him, for Buchanan had been carried fifty feet closer to a brilliantly outlined target that stood conveniently still. The rifle cracked again, in dead earnest, quitting a man named John Riker of all his troubles.

While Buchanan inherited fresh ones — from the house — as two hand guns tried to whipsaw him in a wild fusillade. He threw himself from the bolting, battle-shy horse and ran jackknifed toward the shelter of the porch, ran with such concentration that he was less than a stride from the dangling legs of the lynched Ranger before his startled eyes saw them.

At the same time the porch door swung open and the single-minded Cato came through, dragging the weakly struggling Mulchay. This was the way Gibbons had ordered it, this was the way Gibbons would get it.

"Let him be, brother," Buchanan said, and Cato turned in surprise, as though the gunfight in progress was not supposed to concern him at all.

The knife glinted briefly, started down toward Mulchay's body, and all the off-guard Buchanan could do was swing the rifle, like a club. It hit with a sharp cracking sound, splintering every bone in Cato's money arm, changing the murderous thrust of the blade to a long scratch along Mulchay's chest. Buchanan clubbed him again, to be shed of him, and was primed to resume matters with the pair still inside the house when a moan broke from old Mulchay's throat. It was a mournful little sound, deep, quavering, and spoke of a condition far more critical than Buchanan suspected.

As he bent to scoop the man in his arms a .45 blasted thunderously, slamming its slug into a post exactly level with where his head had just been. It went off again, ripping up the board beside him, but now he had Mulchay in his arms and was seeking the safety of the dark end of the porch. He made it down the steps there, kept going across the side yard and into the sheltering grove beyond.

"There it goes!" Apgar shouted, but Jack Gibbons had already spotted the fire, was already congratulating himself on the military precision, the fine timing of the operation. They were thirty-minutes distant, time aplenty for the flames to do their work, for Cato to do his and all of them be gone — in pursuit of Mexicans, presumably.

Very nice, too, how Malcolm Lord had fallen in with the scheme, how he followed close behind with his own party — just so many more unassailable witnesses to the "enemies'" atrocities.

It was a change from the near-disaster of Seth Keroon's appearance today to the clear triumph tonight — and even up in Austin, though they would suspicion the truth, the situation would make them take heed of Jack Gibbons and tie the governor's hands indefinitely. The Ranger had been strung up by Mexicans. A Mex blade was in Angus Mulchay's heart, his place was gutted by fire — and no less a personage than Malcolm Lord to testify to it.

And when all the poor fools had ridden off, to keep his appointment at the line shack . . . Gibbons suddenly frowned. That fire, he thought, should be growing bigger. What were they doing at the house?

At the house they didn't know what they were doing. Inside the place were Harley

174

and Betters, but they knew only the general plan, hadn't been given anything specific to do as Riker and Cato had.

"Who is that scudder out there, anyhow?" Harley asked when another minute of tight silence had passed.

"The hell with who he is," Betters growled. "I wanna know *where* he is."

"Heard him run off the porch. Damn, I had the son of a bitch cold and he ducked."

"Is Cato dead, or what?"

"He ain't moved."

"Let's go have a look."

"Help yourself."

"What's the matter with you?" Betters demanded.

"I don't like that rifle," Harley admitted. "And what'd Cato ever do for me?"

"For crissake, we can't stay pinned down in here! Riker was supposed to have the house burnin' by now —" He broke off, cocked his head to a noise out front. "What's that?"

It was the sound of wagon wheels, protesting against unaccustomed speed.

"It's the damn scudder," Harley announced. "Hightailin' with the damn buckboard!"

Betters dashed out onto the porch just as Buchanan raced the old wagon abreast of the house. They opened fire at each other on sight, but the moving target eluded Betters. Buchanan's third shot spun the man halfway around, dropped him to his knees. Harley saw that and ducked out of the fire line and threw some token shots after the retreating wagon, but they passed overhead.

The racket ceased as suddenly as it had erupted, and it took a few more moments of it before the idea got through Harley's brain that he was the last able-bodied man on the premises.

"Hey, Betters, you all right?" he called out suddenly.

"Oh, you useless son of a bitch," the voice answered from the porch.

"Watch who you're callin' son of a bitch, buddy."

There was a sound of movement from Cato then.

"Cato!" Harley shouted, crossing to him and kneeling down. "Cato, you hear me? Hey, Cato!" He peered closely. "Jesus — he looks like a mule tromped on him. Cato, can you hear me?"

"Yeah," Cato said then.

"What are we gonna do?" Harley asked him.

The man pushed himself to his hands and

knees and held that position while he moved his head from side to side experimentally.

"You got him, didn't you?" he asked Harley.

"Hell, no, we didn't. What are we gonna do?"

Cato climbed all the way up, looked balefully from Harley to the prone figure of Betters.

"What happened to him?"

"Got plugged. And Riker's dead in the yard."

"Some deal Gibbons worked out," Cato said.

"Do we ride out?" Harley asked.

"Some smart deal," Cato said again, touching his face tenderly, glancing at the figure dangling on the other side of the porch. "Go around and get the fire started," he told Harley. "Then bring the horses."

Harley moved quickly, relieved now that someone was directing things. When he reached Riker he didn't even bother to search for life, just picked the torch from the dust, got it lighted again from the blazing outbuilding and carried it back to the main house. The dry wood took the flame hungrily, noisily, and with a great whoosh the entire roof went up.

He got the horses then, helped boost

Betters into the saddle and the three of them went off.

The last ten minutes had given Jack Gibbons no pleasure at all, but now as the brighter glow appeared in the distance he felt some measure of relief. Whatever the trouble was, Riker had the situation under control. Dependable man, Riker, Gibbons thought, making a mental note to give him a fifty-dollar bonus for the night's work. Something extra for Cato as well, he decided generously.

What a jolt, then, to come upon the smoldering, fire-gutted ruins of Mulchay's house and find Riker a casualty, dead with a bullet hole in his chest — and not to find the damned Mulchay. Gibbons was surveying the perplexing scene in stunned silence when the Overlord party broke upon him.

Billy Neale went directly to the hanging figure on the still-burning porch, risked scorching himself while he cut the man down.

"By God," he said, "it's a Ranger! Those dirty jackals strung up a Ranger!"

"And shot him, both," another rider commented.

"A Ranger?" Malcolm Lord said in a worried undertone to Gibbons. "What was he doing at Mulchay's?"

Gibbons looked at him. "I just got here myself," he said impatiently.

"But Austin will send more. Maybe even troops . . ."

"Then we'll have help fighting Mexicans. Won't have to do it all ourselves."

"Yes," Lord said without enthusiasm. "What is it you're looking for?"

Gibbons stopped craning his head around.

"Looking for any more of my own men," he answered. Apgar had already been sent to scout the immediate vicinity; now he came back, exchanged a glance with Gibbons, and shrugged his shoulders.

Neale walked up to the group.

"They can't be thirty minutes ahead of us, Mr. Lord. What're the orders?"

"The militia will be after them," Gibbons said quickly. "There's nothing Overlord can do now."

Neale looked at him curiously.

"We all want to pitch in here," the cowboy said. "This is everybody's business."

"How do you mean?"

"A neighbor's been burned out," Neale answered simply. "That involves us all."

"Better to leave it to the professionals, Neale," Lord told him, coming into the

179

conversation when it seemed that Gibbons was instructing an Overlord hand. "Well, if there's nothing we can do here, Captain . . ."

"Not a thing."

"Suppose we meet in town tomorrow," Lord suggested.

"In town," Gibbons agreed and the Overlord men moved out.

"Now, by God," muttered Gibbons, "let's find out what happened here." He dismounted, strode to where Riker lay. But for all his anger there was little the dead man could explain to him.

"Betters and him didn't get along none too well," Apgar volunteered. "Could've been a showdown."

"And where's the old man? What did Cato do with him?"

"Don't know."

"Well, God damn it, we've got to find out — and quick! If Mulchay is around loose somewhere, shooting his mouth off . . ."

"And the woman," Apgar said. "You got her in a safe place, don't you?"

There was an insolence in the question that Gibbons would have dealt with swiftly at any other time. But the man was rattled, and wondered himself if she was where he'd left her.

"Beat it into town and tell Kersh what happened. He'll be able to handle it if things get out of control there."

Apgar rode off and Gibbons went to the shack for Rosemarie.

EIGHTEEN

There was a strange and unnatural quiet hanging over Scotstown as Buchanan wheeled the creaking wagon into Trail Street. It's Tuesday night, he told himself; it's a nine o'clock town. But that explanation didn't hold for the tension he could feel, the too-quietness, nor tell him why there were at least a dozen armed men in view on both sides of the street, some walking up and down the wooden sidewalks, some gathered in silent, businesslike little groups.

Suddenly one of the armed men stepped out of the shadows, directly into the path of the horse.

"Hold it, cowboy," he said, grabbing the reins at the bit. "What you haulin' and where?"

Buchanan considered the man, his tone of voice, weighed it against the urgency.

"I'm taking my friend to the doctor's," he said very softly.

"Yeah?" The gunman moved around,

looked into the floor of the wagon at the sightlessly staring, comatose face of Angus Mulchay. "Jesus — what happened to him?"

"I don't know yet. But he needs help." He snapped the reins, but the other one jerked the bit again.

"Go when you're told to, ranny. Now ease that Colt out and hand it over. Also the rifle."

"Come again?"

"This town's under martial law. No unauthorized weapons. Let's have 'em."

Buchanan's tongue had begun to play around his lips, a telltale sign of duress. Then Mulchay moaned, a just barely audible sound.

"Where do I pick 'em up again?" Buchanan asked, giving the handgun over, reaching for the rifle.

"They're stored at the sheriff's, but don't come around for a spell. The lid's on tight."

He was permitted to go then and drove past the familiar building that housed the dancehall, pulled in to the rail before the Glasgow. He pushed through the doors and it was like a wake in there. Ken Hamlin spotted him first.

"Banquo's ghost," the man said, staring.

"I need help for Mulchay. Where's the doctor?"

"That's me," Doc Church said, "but you wouldn't be remembering the last time we met."

"Mulchay?" Hamlin asked.

"He's outside and he's in trouble. Where do you want him, Doc?"

"Terhune has a sofa in back. All right, Terhune?"

"Anything for Angus Mulchay. Bring the man in."

Buchanan did, and cradled in those arms the little man seemed littler still. At a glance they all knew their friend was bad off.

"Set him down soft," Church said, and in his voice there was something very grave. "Hold his head very still." The doctor examined him then, went over his skull, his neck, the vertebrae of his back with knowing fingers that made diagnosis an almost positive certainty. He went back to the neck region again, and something he touched there crowded the dull, myopic expression from Mulchay's eyes, replaced it for a long moment with a look of pain that must have been exquisite. Church had released the pressure in an instant, but still Mulchay's face burned on with some torture he was feeling. His lips parted and he groaned so that each man there winced, felt a terrible thing in the pit of his own stomach.

"Whisky!" Church cried in an agonized voice. "God, bring him whisky!"

It was produced by Terhune, and the doctor saturated his own hand with it, forced his forefinger between Mulchay's clenched teeth. Mulchay's mouth worked, tasting it, and his brain remembered. Church poured some into a tumbler, laid the edge of the glass against Mulchay's lower lip and poured very carefully but unstintingly. Mulchay swallowed, and for another sixty seconds there was no change in his pain-wracked face. Then, almost beautifully, peace came to him. Church poured him another half-ounce.

"Hello, Hamlin," Mulchay said quite lucidly to the face he happened to focus on.

"Hello, Angus."

"I went up to Austin. Saw the governor himself."

"Good thinking, Angus," Hamlin said.

"Came back with a Ranger. Keroon."

"That's fine."

Mulchay started to shake his head but the movement brought on the pain again and Church was ready with the palliating liquor. The eyes became tranquil again.

"What was I tellin' ye, Hamlin?"

"About the Ranger."

"Gibbons killed him. Gibbons and his

dogs shot him down. Have ye seen the lass?" he asked abruptly.

"No."

"Then charge that to his account. It was at MacKay's they struck me down ..."

"The girl is safe," Buchanan said, trying to dispel the awful sadness.

"Buchanan! Is that really you?"

"Keep your head still, Angus," Church cautioned, motioning Buchanan to stand beside Hamlin.

"Ay, there you are!"

"He brought you in," Hamlin said.

"I was wonderin' on that. Seem to recall bein' back at my own place ... mean-faced fella they called Cato ..." The voice kept growing weaker, less intelligible. Abruptly it strengthened. "Doc — do you know when you're going to die? Do you get the damnedest fluttery feelin' across your chest?"

"Some do."

A long sigh went through Mulchay's body. No one spoke or moved. Finally the doctor laid his ear against Mulchay's thin chest, reached at the same time for his wrist. He straightened up, lifted the half-empty tumbler to his own lips and finished it neat.

"He's asleep?" Hamlin asked.

"He's dead. They broke his neck."

"Ahh, what a thing!" MacIntosh said in a choked voice. "What an awful thing . . ."

"Justice!" Hamlin cried out futilely. "We'll have justice for this! Are you with me? Where's Buchanan?" he asked. "Where did the lad go?"

The big man walked through the saloon with his head cast down, eyes studying the sawdust floor. He pushed the doors ajar and stepped into Trail Street, colliding with a passing gunman.

"Watch where the hell you're going, bo!"

Buchanan's head came up.

"You work for Gibbons?" he asked.

"Sure I work for Gibbons."

Buchanan hit him on the point of the jaw and the man went down soundlessly. Two others were attracted by the brief encounter and bore down on him, diagonally. Buchanan bent over the fallen man and very deliberately lifted the .45. The gun in his hand began swinging in a slow arc, exploding six times with a kind of stacatto rhythm until it was empty. He tossed it away from him, negligently, took another from the limp fingers of his nearest victim and started walking down the middle of Trail Street. Twenty-one times he was fired at, six times he answered, and when there was nothing left in that gun he borrowed a third.

On his left was the lighted window of the sheriff's office. He turned and strode toward it behind a murderous stream of fire and lead that shattered the glass and plunged the place into darkness. There had been four men in the office. When he kicked the door in there were two — one dead, one dying. Lou Kersh and the fourth man had fled to the jail in the rear of the building, closed the iron door and bolted it.

What he had seen out there had struck the fear of God into the tough mind of Kersh. For he himself had had his fair chance at stopping Buchanan, had knelt by the sill, nerves under control, gun steady — and watched the man walk right into it, keep coming, coming, coming. Kersh fled.

Now he had his ear to the heavy door and he wondered what Buchanan was doing. What he was going to do. . . .

Buchanan had no idea what he was going to do.

He had looked deep into the dead face of his friend Mulchay and turned away, feeling the long-smoldering rage burst into full flame. He had walked out of the room where Mulchay died for the single, simple purpose of repossessing his property and driving the life out of Jack Gibbons.

Nothing so far had appeased the anger in him. Nothing short of Gibbons would.

And now he had his Colt and his rifle again. Where then was the man? Did he have to hunt him, or would breaking his goddam martial law bring the miserable bastard back here on the run? That seemed the likeliest, and if it was, it left Buchanan with nothing much to do but wait for him.

A sudden storm erupted across the street, from the blacked-out windows of the dancehall, and whining slugs made furious crisscrosses into the walls and the floor and the very desk he was sitting behind. Then a waiting, watchful silence. Buchanan waited with them, the rifle cradled in his arms, and when the target he had chosen made his shoulders a part of the silhouette he took his shot.

A harsh scream, as much dismay as pain, answered. With that, and until they were ordered otherwise, Gibbons' Militia left him strictly alone.

NINETEEN

For the first hour after she had given in to pure exhaustion, Rosemarie slumbered peacefully. But then her sleep became fretful, she tossed and turned on the blanket, cried out several times. All at once she came awake and sat up, looked around at her strange surroundings in disbelief.

"Who are you?" she asked the old man across the clearing.

"Fargo Johns, young lady. And you might as well catch some more sleep. Buchanan's long gone."

It had come back to her as he spoke and now she got to her feet.

"Where do you think you're going?"

"Back down the mountain."

"It'll be dark before you get a third of the way. Better you spend the night here, do your travelin' in the daylight."

"And not know how Tom made out? I'm afraid I'd go out of my mind, Mr. Johns."

"You're liable to get done out of your

life," Fargo said. "Why there's a cat just below this ridge that's over three feet . . ."

"Please — I don't want to hear about it."

"You'll make a great pair."

"What?"

"You and Buchanan, if you ever catch up with him again."

"Catch up? What do you mean?"

"He's quit the mountain for good. Whatever the trouble is down there, when it's settled he's lightin' out."

"Is that what he said?"

"Yep. Gonna stand me a drink in Frisco."

The girl considered that, made no comment.

"Well, I'm off, mister," she said. "Good-by."

"Sure wish you'd wait till morning. Seems foolhardy to go down now."

"I feel I've got to."

"Good luck to you, then."

She waved to him and started down.

When Billy Neale rode out of Mulchay's yard toward Overlord he had the curious feeling he should be going in the opposite direction. There was something very peculiar about Gibbons' behavior, and he was almost certain he had intercepted a signal between the captain and the gunman who rode with him.

"Is that a horse up ahead?" Malcolm Lord asked, breaking into his thoughts. Neale looked up the trail, and sure enough it was somebody's mount — saddled, bridled and riderless. They came up to it, a chestnut mare that eyed them placidly, and Neale inspected her.

"Well, I'll be damned — it's got MacKay's brand!"

"What's it doing this far from home?" Lord asked.

"I don't like it, Mr. Lord. Suppose Rosemarie MacKay was riding her?"

"What would she be riding around here for?"

"Nothing to stop her," Neale said. "Except if she got caught in that raid at Mulchay's . . ."

"Good grief! Then the Mex took her with them."

"If there were any."

"What's that?" Lord asked sharply.

"That raid don't sit right, somehow. That fella comes charging up to headquarters with news Mulchay is being hit. We get close and the fire breaks out."

"Well? That's how the Mex raid, isn't it?"

"So they say. But the Ranger they strung up wasn't killed tonight. He was stiffened out, Mr. Lord. I'd say it happened to him way early in the day."

"That's very possible. They might have come across him anywhere along the river."

"Then why go to all that trouble making it look like it just happened before we rode up?"

"What are you trying to say, Neale? Are you accusing someone?"

"I'm doubling back, boss," Neale said, avoiding a direct answer. "I'm going to look for Rosemarie."

"If the girl is anywhere around, the militia will find her."

"I'm worried about that happening, too."

"Now one damn minute! You know, don't you, that I brought Gibbons and his men into the Big Bend? That I'm responsible for them, and they to me?"

"Mr. Lord, the day Gibbons set foot in this country was the worst thing ever happened to it."

"Watch yourself, Neale — that's insolence!"

"That's truth," Neale replied doggedly. "The man is no good, and that so-called militia is nothing but a hard-case crew. Just so many hired gunnies . . ."

"Draw what's coming to you at the ranch," Lord told him. "You're setting your judgment against mine, and that I can't abide in a hired hand."

Neale shrugged, swept up the mare's dragging reins and took her with him back down the trail toward Mulchay's. The house was just a black, wall-less shell of itself now and he forced himself to make a thorough search of the ruins. There was, of course, no sign of Rosemarie, but he did find a litter of .45 shell casings — a prodigious waste for the ammo-hungry Mexicans along this part of the border — plus a great many cigarette butts in an iron can. Billy had grown up with Mex kids, knew them well, and there was something un-Mexican about this whole deal.

Then, on what had been the porch, he discovered a knife that someone had lost in the shuffle. There was no denying the Spanish look to it, the fancy handle and stiletto-thin blade. He was about to concede the fact of an actual raid when his eyes made out the crude inscription along the shaft. *Brownsville,* it read, *1856.*

That was last year, and last year Black Jack Gibbons was murdering Mexicans in Brownsville. The cowboy wondered if this knife had been taken as loot, kept as a memento.

But even if evidence was growing in his

mind that the raid had been staged, Neale was still concerned primarily with the whereabouts of Rosemarie. He decided that the next place to look would be at her own ranch, and he started off along the river trail at a gallop, hoping in his heart that the girl would be there, safe and sound.

As he neared the place he saw the light of a small campfire, noted that the house itself was dark. He dismounted, led both horses closer. Three men sat around the fire eating, three of Gibbons' Militia, and as he watched, one of them stood up and looked in his direction, as if expecting another arrival. It worried Neale that someone might be coming from his rear, and at that moment a hand touched his shoulder.

"Aren't you Billy Neale, from Overlord?"

"Christ, Mr. MacKay!" he protested, recognizing Rosemarie's uncle. "I liked to have jumped out of my skin."

"Didn't mean to start you, boy."

"Where's Rosemarie?"

"Damned if I know. The girl rode off this afternoon."

"To Mulchay's?"

"No, towards the mountain. Said something about climbing up there for a man."

"Buchanan," Neale said softly.

"Who?"

"A mutual friend," the cowboy said dryly.

"She said Mulchay was being held by that Gibbons fellow. Claimed he was going to be killed . . ."

"So that's the story!" Neale said excitedly, his suspicions confirmed. "And I'll bet it was Buchanan who left the mare there."

"I thought I recognized that horse," Lauren MacKay said. "Say, how does a man go about keeping trespassers off his land these days?"

"The law don't mean much," Neale admitted. "Gibbons does just as he pleases —"

"And right now," a hard voice said, "he's telling both of you to stand fast. I don't need much excuse tonight to kill the pair of you."

"Do as he says, Mr. MacKay," Neale advised him gloomily.

"Cato! Harley!" Gibbons shouted toward the house. "Get down here on the double!"

"Those the ones fighting all the bandits around here?" Neale asked.

"You'll be smart to keep your mouth shut, cowboy."

"Things ain't going off as planned, are they, Gibbons?"

Gibbons swung the gunbarrel viciously, caught Neale behind the ear with it and dropped him unconscious in the dirt.

"How about you?" he asked MacKay ominously. "Any bright remarks?"

"Not me."

Cato and Harley came up and Gibbons turned on them.

"What in the name of God happened back there? How did Riker get shot?"

"Some buck rode up out of nowheres," Harley said. "Just opened up on Riker like that . . ."

"A Mex?"

"Hell, no, he wasn't a Mex."

"What happened to you?" Gibbons asked Cato then, staring at the man's swollen, misshapen face.

"Nothin' I won't fix if I run into him again."

"Was he on the big side?"

"Big enough," Cato answered. "You know him?"

"I think so," Gibbons said. "He took the old man with him?"

"In a buckboard," Harley said. "That's when Betters got winged."

"We'd better get going into town," Gibbons said. "Take these two out back of the house."

"Another fire, too?" Cato asked him.

"Yeah, but do it fast —" Gibbons stopped speaking, turned his head down the trail. "Did you hear something?"

"A horse," Cato said. "In a big hurry."

"Get back out of sight," Gibbons said, slipping his rifle from the boot.

"I hope it's who I think it is," Cato said.

"You," Gibbons said to MacKay. "Stand in the middle of the trail. Wave the rider down."

The hoofbeats grew louder, but there was nothing visible in the blackness down there. MacKay edged out into the center of the roadway, stood with his hands above his head. Then the horse and rider could be seen.

"Wave him down!" Gibbons snapped and the old man moved his arms frantically.

"Go back!" he began shouting unexpectedly. "Go back and get help!" But the horse was being brought up short and it was too late to turn back. Gibbons broke from the shadows and jerked the reins from the rider's hands.

"This is as far as you go," he told Rosemarie. "From now on we'll travel together." He swung to Cato. "Get everybody mounted. We're going to Scotstown."

"I thought you wanted . . ."

"The situation is changed," he said curtly. "Let's move!"

TWENTY

A messenger sent out by Lou Kersh met Gibbons on the outskirts of Scotstown and filled him in quickly on the situation.

"One man?" Gibbons asked with angry derision. "You can't root out one man and finish him?"

"He's holed up now in the sheriff's office. Just sitting behind the desk and picking off anybody that shows his head."

"And what the hell is Kersh doing?"

"Lou says for you to come in and figure something out."

"I will!" Gibbons promised and put spurs to his horse. The oddly assorted party rode into Trail Street noisily, and when it passed the office Buchanan had a swift and disquieting glimpse of the girl riding under guard. He moved out from behind the desk for a better look at this totally unforeseen development, came to stand in the doorway for a moment before three snap shots drove him back inside.

The party dismounted at the Edinburgh Hotel and Rosemarie was taken inside alone by Gibbons and Cato. Gibbons came out of the hotel minutes later, strode briskly and self-confidently across the street to the Glasgow. Hostility toward him in that place fairly crackled with its intensity, but the man glanced from one dark face to another with contempt for all of them in his eyes.

"Where's Angus Mulchay?" he said directly to Hamlin.

"Your business is done with Mulchay," Hamlin said. "He lies murdered in the next room."

"So the bandits killed him, did they?"

"Ay," Hamlin said. "Bandits is as good a name for your gang as any other I've heard."

Gibbons had been pouring himself a drink at the bar. He sipped it now and gazed at Hamlin thoughtfully.

"Talk like that could cost you your life," he said.

"As it cost Mulchay his."

"And there may be many more before this night is done," Gibbons said.

"What are you doing with the lass, Gibbons?" Terhune demanded. "Surely you draw the line somewhere."

"I'm fighting a war," Gibbons told him. "In war you take prisoners. Some prisoners become hostages." He drained the glass, set it down on the bar sharply. "You," he said, pointing to MacIntosh. "Walk up to the sheriff's office. Tell that Mex-lover in there that a man who hates his guts is with the girl right now. Tell him to come out of there with his arms raised or he'll be able to hear her screams. And tell him that Jack Gibbons has never made an idle threat in his life . . ." Gibbons swung around at the sound of the doors swinging open. Malcolm Lord, haggard-faced and haunted-looking, stood there.

"What brings you here?" Gibbons asked brusquely.

"We're through," the rancher said in a toneless voice. "Take your men and ride out."

"Through? I've just begun my work here, partner."

"You're no partner of mine."

"That will be for me to say, when the time comes. What I want you to do is move our herd down to the river grass . . ."

"*Our* herd?"

"I told you I'd get mine," Gibbons reminded him. "One way or another."

Lord turned then to the ring of accusing faces.

"I was hard pressed," the man said to

them, trying to explain. "I needed grass or lose my stock —"

"And you decided to grab Mulchay's," Terhune said. "A fine neighbor, Malcolm Lord."

"I was wrong," he admitted. "I acted badly." He looked at Gibbons again. "But I never condoned the actions you took. Now we're done, Gibbons. Ride out!"

Gibbons was smiling at him.

"I do as I damn please," he said, and suddenly the rancher made an awkward, unfamiliar attempt to clear the gun beneath his coat. Gibbons drew before him, beat him with ridiculous ease and fired two bullets into his body. That brought three of the gunmen into the place and their menacing-looking Colts prevented any more action against Gibbons.

He holstered his weapon, looked around for MacIntosh.

"Tell Buchanan to give himself up," he said and the other man went out of the Glasgow.

His stronghold was now his trap — for hardly had Buchanan seen the girl in Gibbons' hands but he guessed the leverage that would be brought against him. And from a frame of mind where he didn't much care what the hell happened so long as Gibbons got his, now he felt the need to plan beyond that.

The important thing was to get out of here, to find room to maneuver. The metal door behind him was locked tight. The open doorway was being guarded almost jealously by half a dozen snipers across the way. Fifteen minutes ago, if he'd wanted to get out badly enough, he knew he could have made it. But now that the need was here, the cards were abruptly running against him.

Then he heard the footsteps coming along the sidewalk outside.

"Buchanan? Can you hear me, son?"

"Yeah."

"It's MacIntosh, a friend of Mulchay's."

"What's the proposition?"

"A pretty poor one. He's holding MacKay's niece, says the man with her is no friend of yours."

"That covers a lot of sons of bitches now."

"He promises harm to the lass unless you step out with your arms raised —"

"Come on out of your hole, gunfighter!" the shouting voice of Gibbons broke in. "Let's have a look at you!" The shooting of Malcolm Lord and the third jolt of whisky made Jack Gibbons treetop tall. He had it all for himself now — everything.

"Get out of the way, MacIntosh," Buchanan said softly.

"But, man, remember MacKay's niece . . ."

"They're going to open up when I step through. Get yourself clear . . ."

"You've got ten seconds, by God!" Gibbons raged from across the street. "Cato's waiting to cut loose!"

"Not any more he ain't!" cried another voice, and the sound of it made Buchanan blink his eyes.

"Fargo?" he called back.

"The girl's in good hands now, bucko. Just sit tight and wait for a new deal . . ."

"Get that man!" Gibbons bellowed. "On the porch there! Get him — shoot him down!"

A shotgun went off. First barrel. Second barrel. That jayhawk of a Fargo was defending himself, Buchanan thought and started through. Then, from the very corner of his eye, he caught a movement. He whirled with the rifle cradled on his arm and caught Lou Kersh furtively opening the big door. Kersh fired from the hip and the rifle's answer was instantaneous. Kersh dropped dead, but the magic that had been like a coat of armor for Buchanan this night had lost its power. His rib was bullet-grazed and his left side felt numb from the impact.

"Rush the office!" he heard Gibbons ordering outside. "Pour lead in there, you bastards!" And being led again they found their courage again. Across Trail Street they came, ten abreast now, and the rifle that had held them at bay was not going to prevail any longer. Buchanan prudently ducked through the door Kersh had opened, and found himself in the jail. He bolted the door behind him.

It was a large room and contained four separate cells. A dozen Mexicans awaiting execution filled three of them and in the fourth was Tompkins.

"*Oyez, caballeros! Quereis pelear?*" Buchanan invited. "Hey, boys! You want to fight?"

The prisoners did — *con mucho gusto*. Buchanan took the keys from a peg, began opening cell doors. Outside, bullets were beating a tattoo against the metal door.

"I'll fight, too!" Tompkins said. "Just give me a gun!"

A boy of seventeen took Buchanan by the arm, jabbering excitedly and pointing to a locked cabinet. Another key unlocked it, revealing a good size arsenal, and in seconds the eager bandits cleaned it out. The alley door was opened and they poured into the night with a great deal of cheering.

And a cheering sight they were to Fargo and the handful of Scotstowners who had mobilized on the spur of the moment. There was another Greener besides Fargo's, four singleshot Remington pistols and one muzzleloader — and though they diverted six gunmen from the main assault their battle at the hotel was a hopeless one.

Buchanan's bunch hit Gibbons' main force on the flank. Three Mexicans, Tompkins and two militiamen fell in the first exchange, then there was a regrouping, a scattering for protective cover. The six engaged at the hotel hesitated briefly, then turned to add their firepower to the major fight.

But they had reckoned without Fargo.

"Now we got 'em!" he yelled and bounded down the porch steps. Hamlin, Macintosh and Terhune came scrambling after him, as their Highland ancestors would have done, and if their shooting was only sporadic, ineffective, it was still noisy enough to give Gibbons' downstreet group the panicky feeling they were in a vise.

"Let's get the hell out of here!" someone shouted and that did it for them all. They broke and ran in four directions for their horses.

"Cuidado! Cuidado!" Buchanan shouted, worried that the crossfire would hit as many friends as foes. "Watch it!" He himself had crossed to the dancehall, still cradling the rifle, taking his targets as he found them — looking for one in particular.

But it was pandemonium out here now, completely disordered. Something on the ground caught his glance — Gibbons' showy white Stetson. He crushed it with his foot, moved on down an alleyway. There was a burst of gunfire up ahead and he hurried that way. Two of Gibbons' men had a Mexican pinned in a corner, wounded and fighting from one knee. The rifle cut the odds in half and the other one fled.

"Como está, amigo?" Buchanan asked. "How you doing, friend?"

"Bueno," the fellow whispered, *"bueno,"* and lowered himself all the way down to die.

Another spate of shooting beckoned Buchanan and he went that way expectantly. Now it was a pair of Mexicans trying to keep a militiaman from his horse — but not Gibbons, and Buchanan left them to settle it among themselves.

A man's agonized scream split the air, rose grotesquely above the flat sound of guns, made everything curiously personal, somehow. Buchanan was attracted to it, for

no reason he could explain, and found himself at the half-opened side door of the
Glasgow. He stepped into the darkened
storeroom, crossed it and went through a
second opened door that brought him
behind the bar.

Along the bar stood three uncorked bot-
tles, half-a-dozen half-full glasses, a cigar
still burning — a kind of peace that awaited
Hamlin and his friends when the warring
was done . . .

Someone groaned, from the direction of
the private room, and Buchanan moved
around the bar and toward it. He crossed
the threshold. Angus Mulchay lay on the
couch where he had died — but Buchanan
was completely unprepared to find Jack
Gibbons sprawled on the floor within arm's
length of the man he had murdered. Buried
to the hilt in Gibbons' back was a stiletto,
and Buchanan admired the nice little irony
of that.

"Up Scotstown!" cried a voice from the
saloon, startling him out of his thoughts.

"Ay, it's all over but the shoutin'!"

"Drink hearty, lads. Terhune is buyin'!"

Buchanan eased over to the door, looked
in at the bar. They were all there, the
Scotstown Regulars celebrating the victory
over Gibbons' Militia, and in their midst a

fitting replacement for Mulchay.

"I don't believe I've had the pleasure," he heard Hamlin say.

"I'm called Fargo. Fargo Johns."

"You happened by at a fortunate time."

"Happened, my eye! I came down off the mountain a'purpose."

"From the mountain? Then you're partners with Buchanan."

"Was. Anybody seen him?"

"Most likely gone to the hotel to comfort the lass."

"He'll have to get in line then," Fargo said. "When I left her Billy Neale was doin' a fine job."

"Tell me somethin' out of curiosity," Terhune said. "Was it you got her loose from the gunman or Billy?"

"It was him all the way. All I did was get *him* loose from the fella holdin' him."

"They'd make a good family," Hamlin said. "MacKay's niece and the Neale boy."

"Once she gets over her notions about Buchanan. Say — didn't somebody mention a drink? Or was I hearin' things?"

Buchanan grinned, turned from his place at the door and moved across the room. He opened a window and let himself out into the dark night, began walking in search of a stray horse he could borrow. If he rode steady he'd be in Lajitas by tomorrow sun-down. Get himself doctored there and push on.

And this time he was going all the way to San Francisco.